Act I. The Seed on Fire

Michele Sims

Act I. The Seed on Fire. Copyright © 2018 by Michele Sims.

ISBN 978-1-7329031-0-4

Publisher: Green Books Publishers

Editing: Nick May

Cover Design: Select-O-Grafix, LLC

TABLE OF CONTENTS

Michele Sims

CHAPTER ONE

If anyone had told me it was possible for Alicia Tavares Moore to look more beautiful than the first day I met her, or lovelier than the day I made her my wife, I wouldn't have believed it. And I would've been wrong.

At six months pregnant with our first child and glowing, she told me on more than one occasion that she was the happiest she had ever been in her life. Her physical beauty had increased along with the size of her perfectly round and protruding belly. The touch of her skin, silky smooth and warm, sent small shivers down my spine, and its sun-kissed, café-au-lait color was a delight to my eyes. Running my fingers through her styled, chestnut hair, which had gotten thicker and fuller and bounced easily with each step she took, was a privilege I knew not to take for granted. Thinking about her breasts and that behind often caused me to reposition myself in my pants, so I saved those thoughts for private moments. My girl, my wife, my best friend, known as Lecia to most people, was a natural beauty.

I smiled as I thought how grateful I was to live my wildest dreams on top of my game. I had a swank New York apartment and headlined my own small jazz club with my band, Fortune. I had a beautiful wife, and we were expecting our first child. Life couldn't have been better for me, Kaiden Moore, or Cade, as my family and friends knew me.

We were both transplants from Charlotte, North Carolina, and I grew up in a family of three kids. Vincent, my older brother, was without question the family hero and a world-class architect. My sister, Doris, the middle kid, was a famous opera star. My father, Charles Aiden Moore, and especially my mother, Lauren Moore, were quick to remind me that all her children were smart and gorgeous. I was the youngest in the family—seven years younger than Vincent—and for most of my life, I held a comfortable place in his shadow. We shared caramel-brown skin, full lips, dark-brown hair, and broad shoulders, and we were both tall, but unlike him, my first preference was playing the saxophone instead of sports—and I was good at it. We were comfortable in our sprawling home, living in the upscale, southern section of the city known as South Park. Lecia had grown up in a devoutly Catholic family in a larger than modest home closer to Uptown Charlotte in a diverse, close-knit neighborhood.

Everywhere we went—on the streets of Charlotte, and even on the busy streets near Times Square in New York—we heard the same comments. "You're such a beautiful young lady. When is the baby due?" Lecia was always patient and graced them with a bright smile, but her answers to the usual questions only led to more questions.

"Is this your first child?" and "Do you know the sex of your baby?"

What was there for me to complain about? It wasn't like I didn't receive fringe benefits from giving my seed to my wife. She was more than accommodating of my needs for physical contact and was often the one who initiated daily sexual intercourse during her second trimester. Lecia's libido went through the roof as her pregnancy progressed, and I considered it my duty to provide her with relief from her sexual tensions.

"Lecia, is everything alright?" She woke up the following morning and took a little more effort than usual getting out of bed. I noticed she had begun to slow down as she entered the seventh month of her pregnancy.

"Don't you think it's time to start your maternity leave?" I had urged her from the time we'd gotten married to give up her job as a nurse practitioner at a local clinic, but she had refused.

"Cade, they need me. I can't quit now, and besides, I want to work right up until the time of my delivery if I can."

My desire to have my wife at home went unheeded until one day, a child who didn't want to get a shot took a swipe at her baby bump. She fell back against the wall to protect our child from receiving a blow and, without my knowledge of the incident or further urgings to quit, she turned in her letter requesting an extended leave of absence the same day. Lecia was committed to the health and safety of our child, and there wouldn't be a second chance for an incident like that. She sent a message to me that day letting me know she had packed her things and turned in her letter to her supervisor. She and baby bump were waiting for me with a delicious home-cooked meal, sex that satisfied my every desire, and a promise she would not return before the birth of our child. I was in heaven, but I didn't know I was being selfish because I had no intention of sharing my slice of heaven with others.

"Lecia, can we get you something for the baby?" her co-workers pleaded with her after she submitted her letter. Despite my misgivings, she returned to the office for a farewell party/baby shower, resulting in us being inundated with onesies, diapers, assorted baby gear in every color, bunnies, teddy bears, stuffed kittens, action figures, and toy dolls from her team, families of grateful patients, and staff members in other departments. The delivery men started rolling their eyes and giving me sympathetic looks when they dropped off packages on a weekly basis.

As her pregnancy progressed, invitations came pouring in for baby showers from women in her exercise class at the gym, from members of the children's charities she had supported throughout the years, and from former classmates. We had so many things, I felt the baby items had grown like a cancer in the apartment. There were baby items stuffed in every room, every closet, and every space that had a hook, nook, or cranny. It was fun at first to see Lecia's expressions of love for our little one as her belly grew, but the stuff also became a painful reality for me that the presence of a little one in our lives would forever change our relationship.

We had a spacious apartment by Manhattan standards, but we were running out of space with so many gifts; Lecia started placing the overflow in my home office. I couldn't find my musical arrangements, my space was in constant disarray, and the flow of my creativity was interrupted by tigers, lions, and bears staring at me. I felt like I was being crowded out of my own home, and I refused to have more baby things invade my space. I needed to make my position clear.

"Lecia, while I appreciate the generosity of others, enough is enough. We don't need more baby things." I gave her my best puppy-dog look, hoping I could elicit a little sympathy. She always told me that I had her at day one, if she was being honest, when I looked at her with my gorgeous brown eyes and my pouty lips—her description, not mine. I thought I was making my point and being as gentle as possible in approaching this delicate subject.

"Why do you have to be so unreasonable Cade?"

Her voice trembled, and I could see the color rising in her cheeks before she burst in an unexpected torrent of tears. I watched, mouth wide open, and remained silent as she blubbered through her response.

"Kaiden, this has been the happiest time of my life—so what if we have to deal with a little inconvenience?" Her chest heaved, and I could hear her labored breath. "Life isn't always going to be convenient Cade, and who ever said it needed to be in order for us to be happy?"

I wasn't sure where she was going with this, so I shrugged.

"Is it convenient that we have to wake up each morning to hammering and the sound of electric saws buzzing from the construction going on next door? No, but we do it. The work crew has been coming earlier in the morning and staying later at night."

"Lecia, I did get in touch with the owner of the building and he said he couldn't place me in touch with the Turlingtons, who own the apartment next to us. They're out of the country and he couldn't give us their contact information. You know the terms of our homeowners' contract state that our privacy must be guarded, but there's good news. We've been given a large discount for nine months on our homeowner fees for our inconvenience." I smirked as the last word rolled off my tongue.

Lecia pursed her lips and rubbed her belly, which always turned on her smile, but it faded when she spoke. "That's good to know now that I'm not contributing to our monthly income."

"Lecia—" I huffed, and she waved her hand in the air to cut me off.

"I know you're going to say we're not hurting for money and you prefer that I stay home, but since I've been away from work, I've been getting phone calls every day from Darlene, which I haven't returned, as if she has conveniently forgotten we're no longer friends. She left a message yesterday asking me if our friendship ever meant anything to me. She said she was sorry for her part in the way our friendship ended, but she didn't miss a beat to remind me that it was my choice to fall in love with you and marry you even though I knew she had feelings for you."

My head tilted back from the weight of hearing this old discussion for the umpteenth time. Yes, Darlene had a fan crush on me, and yes, I had a serious crush on her former best friend—my Lecia. I've never regretted following my heart and making Lecia my wife. Two years later and this was still a landmine for me. I sighed and decided to tread with caution.

"Lecia, Darlene was once your friend, and I agreed with the decision to let you handle the situation with her. You know the two of you can never be friends again. She said she forgave you, for what I don't know, but the woman started throwing shade at you at work after we moved in together and tried to turn the other nurse practitioners against you— but they could see through her. They know that you're the nurse practitioner Darlene wishes she could be, and she'll never again find a friend as good as you were to her. This is just Darlene trying to play more mind games with you."

Lecia took one of the teddy bears thrown on the couch near her and placed it in her lap.

"I know in my head that Darlene and I could never be friends again, but it's hard feeling the same thing in my heart. She and I started nursing school together, and we've been there for each other throughout our careers. I miss the collegial relationship that grew into a genuine friendship. Darlene is lonely, and I guess it was loneliness mixed with lust for you that doomed our relationship. I know her heart is a lonely hunter and it won't let her be happy for us." She bit her lip and was on the verge of tears when I got up and took her into my arms.

"If that's true, then you should be concerned that jealousy is the poison that makes the arrows of the hunter more potently dangerous. I'm begging you to stay away from her Lecia, and there's nothing like determination followed by deliberate action to help us move forward. I've told you before, just block her number from your contact list. You don't need the drama, and tomorrow—not next week or next month, but tomorrow—we can call the charity of your choice and just get rid of most of these stuffed animals." I tried to take the teddy bear out of her lap that was blocking my attempt to rub her belly and feel the baby's movements.

"Let it go Cade. I said I would take care of the toys, and I will." She tried to push away from me.

"Lecia, I hear you, but it seems to be getting worse." I could feel the emotional landmines exploding all around me.

"I can't do this with you now Cade." I tried to reach out to comfort her, but she pulled back and moved further away from me.

"Lecia, we need to talk about this."

"No, we don't need to talk when you're trying to ruin what should be a fun time for us. I'm home like you wanted, and we've spent more time together in the last few weeks than we've had in the last year. You're not touring, and I'm not away on call at the hospital." She eventually threw her hands up in frustration and left the room, with me feeling more confused and bewildered than I had been at the beginning of our discussion.

I got up, started putting away the dishes in the sink, and then went to my study. Lecia came in the room, where I was seated at my desk in front of a blank sheet of music, holding my head in my hands and surrounded by the menagerie looking at me. I swore the elephants and bunnies had frowns of disapproval on their faces.

"I was just being hormonal." She came closer and placed her hands on my shoulders as I placed my hands around her and kissed her swollen belly, which moved under my touch in a slow wave.

"I promise I'll give some things to charity and maybe auction off some to help mothers who aren't as fortunate." I rose and kissed her full, soft lips in appreciation. She stroked my cheeks, and it helped that she was attempting to see my point in all of this.

"I wasn't trying to be difficult. I just need a space to call my own. Thanks for being understanding, and I never meant to upset you." I stared deeply into her eyes.

"You know Cade, with your good looks and those eyes, you can scorch the panties off me. I know you weren't trying to be mean."

We kissed, and I walked her to our bedroom, where we made up with hours of love and sex. We were cool for a week following our makeup sex session, but I couldn't erase the gnawing feelings that maybe we hadn't had enough time together as a married couple before we found ourselves expecting our first child. Lecia and I had lived together for over a year, but she'd gotten pregnant on our honeymoon, and we'd started our married life as a threesome. I thought I was being humorous when I jokingly shared my concerns about being a parent so soon with her, but she wasn't having it.

"We're blessed to have the chance to share our love with a child—a child we made together." That was the end of the discussion and time to move on.

"Lecia, do you need an assistant to help you sort through the baby items?" I asked on my way out the door to the club. The baby's things weren't disappearing at a steady pace; instead, more baby items were being delivered. I kept my face as neutral as possible.

"You handle things at the club and I'll take care of things here." Her hair was high on her head and she was dressed in her plush white robe when she came to kiss me at the door and slowly walked away with her hand on the small of her back.

"Goodbye Cade." I felt dismissed.

Michele Sims

CHAPTER TWO

I arrived at the club earlier than usual and walked to my office, past the wall lined with pictures of the band early in the game and of artists on their way up in the world of jazz. This was my world, and I breathed a sigh of relief after I opened the door and turned on the lights.

"Everything is just as I left it," I said it loud and boldly, hoping the forces in the universe could hear that every man needed his space. My phone buzzed with a text and I knew before looking at the screen who it was from.

Vincent: In the parking lot. ETA two minutes.

Vincent and I had agreed to meet for an early breakfast today, as we had done over the years, and because he needed to make contact with one of the operatives of the organization he had been a member of since his mid-twenties—The Network, an international, highly organized intelligence agency of agents and operatives where people of power, politicians, military leaders, captains of industry, mercenary soldiers, and those from all walks of life have come together to achieve goals that affect all mankind. What were these goals? Vincent said he would have to shoot me if he revealed them to me and—he was serious.

I had been enlisted as a courier, the nameless average New Yorker, to drop off packages, give code words to waiters in upscale restaurants, and to enjoy walking a dog on loan to me in the park. I would have done anything for Vincent. Hell, I loved and admired the guy. He knew I had his back and wouldn't ask questions, so when he asked me to use the club as a cover, I was on board. As I got older and wanted a little more action, I learned more about the shadowy, secret group, its budget loosely estimated by Vincent in the billions, with a worldwide group of analysts and "contractors." No one on the planet was beyond the reach of the Network. If you had a birth certificate, fingerprints, or a picture taken of you at any time in your life, the Network could find you.

My phone buzzed again, and it was the delivery guy from our favorite deli with our breakfast. I went to the back door to grab our food before Vincent arrived.

"Thanks Cal. I can always depend on you to be prompt." He gave me the bag and the carton containing our coffees: dark roast, no sugar.

"You bet Cade. Boss says you're one of our best customers. Today it must be only you and your brother. I delivered enough food last night to this place to feed an army. I placed the order on your tab and you can settle your bill at the end of the month as usual. By the way, thanks for the tips. You're one generous guy."

"Sure thing Cal. See you later." *Must have been a meeting for the Network operatives last night.* I wasn't ever in on those meetings, and Vincent always made sure the food bills were paid.

I watched as Cal returned to his truck and waited a few minutes but saw no signs of Vincent, so I headed back to my office; and seated on the couch was my brother.

"What took you so long? I told you I was close by." He took a cup of coffee and waited for me to hand him a sandwich.

"I was looking for you at the back door?" I frowned and sat down, unwilling to be interrogated first thing in the morning.

"I never enter or exit the same way twice. I told you man—you've got to learn to vary your path." He took a sip of his coffee.

"Your mind is warped Vincent. You see danger around every corner." I unwrapped my sandwich and smelled the aroma of the ham and melted cheeses.

"I had oatmeal with Lecia this morning, but this sandwich...this is what I call breakfast."

"I hear you man. Your guys were here jamming until late out front, which gave us the noise and distraction needed to meet with the operatives last night. You don't know how much you're helping us with a mission here in the city."

"I should thank you. When we were on tour your operatives gave the band a completely different sound, masquerading as back-up singers and additional band members. Where did you recruit them?" Vincent's eyes narrowed, and he threw me a cold, steely glance.

"My bad. Forget that I asked, but they were good, and the fact that the Network paid their salaries and covered their expenses—I say the deal was mutually satisfying."

"Good. I'll let you know if we need any of them to accompany you on your next tour. Enough about that, how are things with you and Lecia?"

"Fine." I filled my mouth with bread and meat, hoping it would give him pause before asking too many questions.

"Seems that there's more to it. You said it too fast; and filling your mouth with food has never stopped me from getting into your business." I grabbed a napkin and wiped my mouth.

"You're exactly right. It's my life and my business, but there is something I wanted to talk to you about."

"Yeah?" He was always willing to help where he could.

"You remember my neighbors, the Turlingtons? Well, they're travelling overseas but are having major renovations to their apartment while they're away. I can sleep through anything, but the noise over the last six months is starting to get to Lecia. I wanted to contact them, and the building owner said he couldn't help me. Do you think the Network could help?" Vincent laid down his sandwich.

"If you're asking if the Network could find the Turlingtons, the answer is yes. The business of the Network has always included giving a weight to any investigation of the enemies of the organization and to its specific interests. I'm afraid, brother, that finding the Turlingtons doesn't rise to the level of significance for the Network. It can't afford to take unnecessary risks of exposing its existence, and besides, how would you explain how you tracked them down and who gave you the information?"

"You have a point, but I thought it was worth asking you, for Lecia's sake."

"Yes, for Lecia's sake I think we're talking about something more here. I suggest you keep it real with her about the baby. She's told Dana that she has been losing sleep worrying about how the baby is affecting you. It's natural to have concerns, especially about your first child. Having a baby is a life changer."

"I've gotten to the point that I'm cool about the baby, but the fact that our home is turning into one big nursery is what's bugging me."

"Here's another piece of advice. Let Lecia enjoy the experience of her first pregnancy, baby stuff and all. I promise, these things have a way of working themselves out."

"You seem so sure about it. Is there something you're not telling me?" I looked him straight in the eye.

"Call it experience, that's all. Dana told me before I left home that she and Lecia were getting together to go shopping."

"Shopping? I'm going to blow a gasket if she comes home with another lion, tiger, or teddy bear." A head of steam was starting to build inside my head, and I picked up my horn from its stand and blew a mixed melody of my frustration, excitement and fears.

"Sounds good bro. You should consider placing that on a new track and calling it, Daddy's blues." He picked up his sandwich and took the final bite.

Michele Sims

CHAPTER THREE

"Lecia, are you home?" All the lights were off, and the apartment was quiet.

I walked down the hall and into the darkened practice room where I played my compositions. Turning on the lights, I saw a crib, rocking chair, and baby outfits in my space. We had agreed to make the smallest bedroom the nursery and keep my room intact. My instruments, and the drafting table complete with the compositions I had slaved over for weeks, were gone. There was no other way to describe my response. I went ballistic. I fisted my hair in my hands, then slapped the wall, hoping the physical pain would diminish my emotional anguish. It didn't.

Pacing through the apartment, I didn't feel the pain of my sore hand or tired feet as I tried to get a grip on things and calm down. I didn't want a repeat waterfall of tears by saying the wrong thing to Lecia, so I decided to get a drink and sit in the bedroom, where she had cleared some of the mountains of baby stuff. I started pacing again but, I was making multiple trips to the bar to refill my glass and returning to the bedroom, where I would sprawl across one of the chairs until the time to get the next drink. I turned the lights out when I looked in the direction of the bed and saw even more stuffed animals peeking from behind the headboard.

I heard the sound, of keys turning the lock and Lecia's voice as she entered the apartment, accompanied by folks who sounded like my older brother Vincent and his wife, Dana.

"Cade are you here? I'm home." Sounds of laughter, footsteps, and lights clicking on invaded the apartment, but by that time, I was wasted and on my second bottle of scotch. She came around the wall that separated the space from the entryway and found me sitting in a deep cushioned chair, where I had moved to be closer to the bar.

"Hi babe. Vincent and Dana are here." She walked into the room and gave me a kiss on the cheek.

"Eeww." She wrinkled her nose and fanned away the fumes of alcohol that I guessed was assaulting her nose and causing her eyes to water.

"Hey Cade." Vincent and Dana came in, and I gave them a side-eye look as I saw them look at each other when I didn't return their greetings.

"Cade are you alright?" I could hear the concern in Lecia's voice, but when I looked in her eyes, filled with the scorn of judgment, I became more irritated. A deep frown spread across my face in a counter move as I looked up at her and squinted, not trying to veil my anger. My lips were drawn painfully tight, and in my drunken rage, I refused to answer her question. I felt so misunderstood by the woman I loved more than life itself, and I needed to get out of here before I said something I would later regret. The floor seemed like it was moving as I got up from my chair and tried to steady myself on wobbly feet. Seconds later, I wasn't sure why I was talking, but it was my slurred voice that filled the room.

"I'm your husband, Lecia. Have you forgotten that? Are you trying to push me out of your life?"

"Cade, what are you talking about?" She took a seat on the couch and began rubbing her belly while Dana took a seat next to her, narrowing her eyes at me. I looked at the chair across the room and noticed it too was filled with stuffed animals, which further enraged me. I stumbled toward the colorful zoo of smiles and tossed them on the floor. Lecia said nothing more to me even though I waited for her response. Instead, she and Dana looked at each other with open mouths in total silence. Vincent came closer to me to block my view of Lecia and I'm sure to block her view of me. I was in a sad state, and the truth was I felt overwhelmed, with scary thoughts running through my head—that I may not be ready to be a father. I placed my hands on the sides of my head and covered my ears. Lecia had begun crying, and I didn't want to hear more sobs or anything Vincent had to say.

"Cade calm down. Let's go in another room and talk."

Why did he say that? My vision blurred and narrowed, and I couldn't see anyone or anything in the room as I struggled to form coherent thoughts.

"What room would you suggest Vincent? Would you like to go to my study or my composition room? Oh, I forgot, they are now a nursery and clothes closet for the baby. I don't have a place in my own home anymore." He extended his hand to me, but I stumbled to my feet and started walking without his assistance while he followed me to the back of the apartment. Lecia was still crying, and I heard her tell Dana she should go home and check on their four children.

"I'll be ok." Her sobbing was tearing through me, leaving me feeling raw.

"Lecia, I don't want to leave you while you're so upset." Dana tried comforting her.

I stopped in the hallway, frustrated I had messed up again, and I turned around to see Vincent walking back toward his wife and Lecia.

"Dana, take the car home and I'll find a way back after I talk to Cade. Don't worry, I just need to talk out some things regarding this situation with my brother."

Dana looked at Vincent teary eyed and hesitated before hugging Lecia and gathering her things.

Hmm, I guess I've created a situation. I fought to keep the walls that seemed to be vibrating in various colors from making me nauseous. Vincent came back to talk to me, and I didn't want to fight with him, so I followed him, staggering along the way, to another room in the apartment.

"Cade, this isn't like you. Speak to me man. I know it's hard getting used to all the changes, but I've been there and maybe I can help." He placed his hand on my shoulder. I didn't reply to him but tried to push his rock-hard body to the side. I wasn't so far gone that I forgot he was an award-winning wrestler in college and could handle my ass if he wanted to. I was glad when he eventually moved aside and didn't try to block my path.

"I need to go and apologize to Lecia. I need to tell her I'm sorry." I headed out of the room and, as we got closer to the kitchen, I stopped and overheard her talking to her friend Marco Rodriguez on speakerphone. Marco was an old boyfriend who lived in Charlotte, North Carolina, and she was crying as she spoke to him.

"I don't think Cade wants the baby. He's angry most of the time now as my delivery date gets closer, and I won't burden him with a child he doesn't want."

"Lecia, you know I never stopped loving you. Let me come get you and I'll take care of you and the baby. We can raise him or her as our own child."

Vincent was quiet as I looked back at him while we both overheard the conversation. He pushed me forward, but my feet stayed planted where I stood just outside the kitchen. My legs weren't wobbling, but I wasn't moving closer to Lecia either. I did want my child, but before I could stake my claim, I heard words that shook me to my core.

"I don't know how much more of this I can take. I'm more on edge, and this can't be good for the baby. I don't know if I should stay." Her words sounded strangled in her throat, but she said them, and I heard them.

"I'm here for you Lecia, just say the word and I'll be there."

Marco was urging my wife to leave, but she remained silent, pondering his offer, until she relieved my fears with her answer.

"I'm not leaving my husband for another man. That's not what I want or need."

I was still frozen in place, but Vincent came from behind me and entered the kitchen.

"Lecia, can you end your call so we all can talk?" His voice was calm and soothing, and I knew I was at a tenuous point in my relationship, but my brain was too drunk to form coherent words to improve my standing with my wife. I sensed Vincent knew this too, and on one level I resented his interference, but the rational part of my brain trying to come from under the fog of an alcoholic stupor knew that Lecia was the best thing that had ever happened to me and that I needed all the help my brother could render. She was still holding the phone in her hand, and Marco resumed staking a claim to her—though she was no longer his.

"Lecia, who are you talking to? Are you safe? Let me come get you."

Vincent took the phone from her, slowly and gently. She turned her head from me but not before I saw a pained look of fright as she shook her head in confusion. Her hands were shaking, and she leaned against the counter for support while

Vincent ended the call without saying anything to Marco. He moved closer and took her into his arms to comfort her. Neither one of them was focused on me as I turned and staggered away from the scene of my wife crying in the arms of one man and seeking comfort from yet another man. I didn't say anything about her talking to Marco, who had disrespected me in my own home, because I was angrier at myself than anyone else. Although I was deeply in love with my wife, I was the one who had disrespected myself as a man by turning to alcohol to drown my problems instead of dealing with them. I wanted my child, and I wanted the old relationship I once shared with Lecia—the relationship where I could tell her anything, including things she didn't want to hear, and we always worked through our differences. This time it was different. When I had shared my uncertainties about being a father with her last week, our relationship had chilled, and since that time, all hell had broken loose.

I was just being honest, and haven't we appreciated each other's honesty in the past? What is happening to the two of us?

I couldn't deal with the picture unfolding before me in real time any longer. I left them in the kitchen and went to get my jacket. Grabbing my keys, I found my way to the door and stumbled out of the apartment.

I'll get a cab and go back to the club. Yeah, that's what I'll do.

I opened the door and slammed it behind me, but no one came to pursue me. I walked away alone to deal with the demon of jealousy.

Act I. The Seed on FIre

I awakened the next morning in my office at the club, where I'd spent the night sleeping off the effects of too much alcohol. Gathering my strength, I resolved I needed to talk to Lecia. It was still early, and most of the staff had not arrived to break the silence of my surroundings. Things seemed clearer to me alone with my thoughts and surrounded by my first love: my music. She loved me no matter what, and my music made me feel good when I was sad; she provided me with the melody of relief that no matter what happened, it would be alright. My music had been my one and only lady love until I'd met Lecia, and right now I needed to hold her, to receive her affirmation. I went to the bathroom, cleaned myself up, and took a cab back home.

What's going to happen when I open this door? I wasn't sure, but I knew it wasn't going to get any better if we didn't talk about things, so I placed my keys in the lock and slowly opened the door to our darkened apartment. The jangling of my keys and the thump of my wallet echoed the actions of my heart as I threw them on the table in the hall.

"Lecia, are you home? It's me. Lecia, where are you?"

An uneasy weighted feeling settled in my chest as I sensed she wasn't here. The stuffed animals were still scattered on the floor where I'd tossed them the night before. I went to our bedroom and walked quietly so as not to wake her if she was still asleep. Several drawers of her dresser were opened, as was the door to her closet, and the light from the space shined into the bedroom. I went to inspect her closet and discovered more than a few articles of her clothing had been removed from the hangers, and some of the hangers had been tossed on the floor as if she had grabbed her things in a hurry. Pairs of shoes were missing, and her favorite pocketbook was gone. My heart started beating rapidly, and my skin was heated and moistened with beads of sweat as I looked around the room. The bed was still made, with all the pillows still neatly in place. I ran my hands through my hair. It appeared as if Lecia hadn't spent the night at home.

I looked on the night tables on both sides of the bed and there was no note for me. I checked my phone and she hadn't attempted to contact me. I called her phone and the call promptly went to voicemail. There were no words to describe my feelings as a pall of sadness descended upon me. I walked to the front of the apartment, sat down on the couch with my head in my hands, and cried bitter tears. There was no need to fool myself, she was gone.

What have I done?

No one had to tell me I'd screwed up. As my tears fell, I already knew it. I also knew that I didn't measure up to my brother, the proud father of four who could have easily won a Father of the Year award from any organization. I had always known that Marco was still in love with Lecia, but even though I'd been jealous last night, I knew she was no longer in love with him. What I didn't know was how to fix the situation. *How can I make things right between us?*

Man up Cade, I told myself as I wiped away my tears and called Dana. She picked up the phone immediately.

"Hey, have you heard from Lecia? I'm home and she's not here."

"I haven't talked to her since last night, but if she calls, I'll tell her to call you. Have you tried calling her?"

She knew I had.

"Yeah, but my call went to voicemail and she hasn't returned my call yet."

"Don't worry. If she calls me, I'll call you and at least let you know she's alright."

"Thanks Dana. I'll talk to you later."

I could hear the concern in her voice as she tried to reassure me. Knowing Dana, she was probably trying to contact Lecia right after we hung up. I thought about calling her parents in North Carolina, but I didn't want to worry them. I made the decision to stay home tonight and wait for her to contact me. I called my band members and made up an excuse for missing practice.

Lecia and the baby were my priority. We were still in love with each other, and I could only pray she understood the reasons for my behavior last night at least enough to forgive me. I got up off the couch and began picking up the stuffed animals and arranged them as best as I could. I didn't want her to come home to a mess, and I promised myself to do anything I could to make things right between us.

Michele Sims

CHAPTER FOUR

A day passed, and I was worried that I hadn't heard from her. I knew she spoke to her parents daily, and I clung to the fact that she was still in contact with them. Otherwise they would have called me if something was wrong or if they hadn't heard from her. She just needed some time, and as hard as it was to not stalk her, I tried to give her the space she must have needed. I called Dana again.

"I haven't heard from her either and this isn't like Lecia to not return my calls Cade. She's not angry with me; she's disappointed in you."

"No need to spare my feelings Dana. Tell me how you really feel."

"You know I love you both Cade, but I'm worried about Lecia. She wasn't in a good place the last time we talked, and it's not good for the baby."

"I feel you Dana, and I'm giving her one more day. If she doesn't contact me, I'm calling her parents. I feel she's still in contact with them."

"Okay Cade but let me know if you hear from her."

My concerns were mounting, and to bind my own anxiety, I sent messages and called her so many times, I lost count. My night was bad, and I tossed and turned before finally getting out of bed to call Lecia again.

"Hello Lecia, I love you. Please call me back. I'm worried about you, about us. You don't have to forgive me just yet, but I need to know you're okay. Bye, I love you and the baby."

Her response remained the same: nothing. No return phone call and no attempts to reach out to me through others. I wasn't going to stop until I made her talk to me today because although I was wrong by causing this separation, I deserved to know she was alright.

My coffeemaker hummed as I took a break to get another cup of strong brew to keep me awake, and my phone began ringing, causing my hand to tremble; either from drinking a third cup of coffee or with the anticipation it was Lecia. I fumbled with the phone, shaking in my hand, and pressed the accept call button.

"Lecia, baby, is that you? Are you alright?"

"No Cade, it's Marisela." It was Lecia's mother. My heart dropped in the pit of my stomach with the uncertainty of what I was about to hear.

"Lecia kept telling me her phone's battery was dead and she promised me she was going to call you, but I knew if she had contacted you, I would have received a phone call from you by now, at the very least asking about her father's condition."

"What's wrong with Aridio? What happened? No, Lecia hasn't called me." I blinked in surprise at hearing that something was wrong with Lecia's Papi.

"He fell off a ladder and has a broken leg, a head injury, and he's still in a coma. The doctors aren't sure of the extent of his injuries currently, and they're still conducting tests. Lecia hasn't left her father's bedside, and I told her she needed to rest but she won't leave the hospital. I thought you needed to know what's happening here in Charlotte. Are things alright between you and mija?" I let out a breath of relief.

"Thank you, Marisela. Of course I'm concerned about you and Aridio. You're my family and yes, Lecia and I are dealing with some issues right now, but I'm trying to give her some space."

"Cade, I'm worried that the issues between the two of you may have something to do with Marco. I heard him tell Aridio last week that he was still in love with Lecia, and he has been here at the hospital to see Aridio, but I knew he was more interested in seeing Lecia. When will you be able to come to Charlotte?"

"I'll be there tonight." I sighed and smiled, grateful to know Lecia was alright.

"Thank you, Cade. Lecia may not be willing to accept this, but she needs you and your child needs you. I think she's putting her health at risk by staying at the hospital. Mija is a strong woman, but the truth is she's afraid. She's worried she may lose her father, and we're all worried about him, but we don't want her to place her health in danger. She won't be able to survive this if something happens to the baby, and Aridio will only blame himself if he finds out she wasn't taking care of herself. He's looking forward to the birth of his first grandchild, and I believe he's so stubborn, he'll hold on to be here for the baby. You can't imagine what your baby means to our family."

"Don't worry Marisela. I haven't admitted it before, but I've had anxieties about us being parents for the first time and I haven't handled it well. Lecia must forgive me for not being there to support her, and I plan to make her understand that it was just my fears talking. I'll be leaving New York on the first flight out. Thanks for calling me, and I love you Marisela. I'm praying for Aridio and I'll be there for you. Goodbye."

"I love you too Cade. See you soon. Goodbye."

I hung up and began packing for possibly the most important trip of my life. I called Vincent before leaving

New York to let him know about Lecia. I knew he was concerned about me and my family.

"Hello Vincent, this is Cade. I'm flying out to North Carolina to be with Lecia and her family. Her mother called and said Lecia's father had a bad fall off a ladder and is in the hospital in a coma."

"Hey and thanks for calling bro. Dana and I were worried about Lecia. It's too bad what happened to her father, but at least we know where she is and that she's safe. Dana and the children are in Charlotte for the weekend visiting our parents and I'm planning to leave for Charlotte tonight after my consultation with a client."

"Alright, I'll catch up with you down there. I plan to leave on the first flight out. Talk to you later."

"Later brother. Have a safe flight."

"You too, goodbye."

"Bye Cade."

Vincent had handed over the reins of running his architectural firm on a day-to-day basis to his successor after he made the decision years ago to focus on rearing his growing family. He still met with his employees in consultation and as the lead architect on the major contracts. I hung up the phone and refused to let my thoughts dwell on my brother right now. I didn't want to start ruminating on the fact that I was concerned I wouldn't measure up and become as good a father to my child as he was to his children. It was just another possibility I had to accept. I'd grown up in my brother's shadow, and fatherhood could just be another light focused on my deficits.

I'm a musician, a composer and a decent vocalist but not the golden child or the perfect man. There were things I was better at than Vincent, and our father had provided us with a good example of parenting a child, but maybe I was too selfish to pass on those lessons to my own child. I couldn't worry about that now. I had to get to Lecia.

I arrived in Charlotte after a delay of the evening flight and caught a cab to the hospital. I wasn't looking forward to the prospect of Marco sitting by my father-in-law's bedside comforting my wife, but I had prepared on the plane for that probability since I needed to maintain my composure if he was there. I stopped at the nurses' station, and they directed me to his room at the end of the hall. I walked into the room and there were machines beeping and wires everywhere. The smell of antiseptic solution permeated the air and hung like a sign announcing that sickness and death had a foothold in the place. I shivered as I got my first look at Papi lying in bed with his eyes closed and there was Lecia sitting in a chair next to her father's bedside alone, with Marco nowhere in sight. A tear dropped from her eyes as she clenched his hand and stroked it as if willing him to cling to life. She started praying while I remained in the doorway, not wanting to interfere with her intercession with her heavenly father praying for the life of her beloved Papi.

"Dios mio,
All our times are in thy hands,
All diseases come at thy call,
and go at thy bidding.
Thou redeemest our lives from destruction,
and crownest us with thy loving kindness,
and tender mercies.
We bless thee that thou has heard our prayers,
and commanded deliverances for my Papi,

that he may be healed. Amen."

She crossed herself and looked up at me coming into the room, but she made no effort to come to me or to speak. Her posture stiffened as I got closer to her, and with her shoulders slouched low in the chair, she stroked her father's hair and resumed her vigil at his bedside.

"Hi Lecia," I got close to her, taking care not to upset her by forcing her in my arms.

"Hello Cade." She looked tired and drawn from sleepless nights, and I stopped behind her chair and touched her shoulder before coming around to face her and help her to her feet and into my arms. She didn't resist me, but she didn't respond to my embrace, nor to the tender kiss I placed on her lips. I placed my hand on her belly and caressed my child growing inside her.

"Your mother called me Lecia. I was so worried about you when you didn't return my calls." She took in a full breath and let out a deep sigh.

"Mami told me she called you and I didn't mean to worry you, but I was preoccupied trying to be here for Papi." Her response was brief, followed by more silence. She pulled away from my embrace and, sitting back down at her father's bedside, she shifted her focus back to him. I looked at him with sad eyes, seeing such a vibrant man so full of vigor now lying motionless in bed except for the slow rise of his chest. His eyes remained closed and he had bruising on the side of his face.

"How is he?" I placed my hand on his.

"We're not sure. He's holding his own."

"Lecia, can I get you something? Is Marisela coming back soon, so we can go somewhere and talk?"

"I convinced Mami to go home by promising her I would leave in the morning when she returned to the hospital. She needed to rest in her own bed. I'm sure she didn't tell you she had been keeping a bedside vigil before I arrived."

One of the nurses came in and spoke to us and I pulled up a chair to listen.

"Hi Kate, any news from his doctor?" Lecia looked up at her and gave her a faint smile.

"No, nothing new to add Lecia. Your father's vital signs have remained stable, and right now, he's holding his own. The good news is his condition has been upgraded from critical to serious but stabilizing."

"That's good news." Lecia let out a breath and I embraced her for support.

"Is this your husband, Lecia?"

"Yes, this is my husband Cade Moore, and you can speak candidly in front of him."

"Pleased to meet you Kate. I just got in from New York and I'm trying to wrap my head around this. My father-in-law has always been an energetic man. It's good to hear his vitals have stabilized."

"Yes, it is. We were happy when his blood pressure started coming down and I wish I could tell you more, but his doctors will be in to see him early in the morning."

"Thank you for sharing the good news," Lecia responded as we both watched Kate adjust the settings on his monitors before she left us alone in the room.

"Lecia, come home with me and I'll bring you back in the morning." I placed my hands firmly on her shoulders, but this time she stiffened her back and withdrew in response to my touch.

"I can't do this with you today, Cade. I don't want to argue, and I don't want to talk about us right now. Don't you understand I need to be with my father? I plan to keep my promise to go to Mami's, where I left my things, and get some rest tomorrow, so don't worry and you don't have to come back in the morning. I'll be alright...before I forget, I plan to talk to Dana this weekend about moving the baby's things out of the apartment. Papi will have a long road to recovery and I want to be here for him."

"Lecia, I didn't come here to upset you and don't worry about the things in New York. That's not important right now." She turned her back to me and began stroking her father's hair. I leaned in and kissed her on the side of her face.

"I can stay here with him, so you can get some rest—or I can stay here with you."

"No Cade, I want this time with my father. We need this time and I want to make sure he knows I'm here. Do you know my father never left my twin brother's bedside until the day he died? He died before our fourth birthday. I want to do the same thing for him. I need to be here."

"Lecia, he's getting better. We don't need to worry about losing him."

"Cade do this for me at least for tonight. Go to your parents' home and we can talk tomorrow."

"I know when you've made up your mind Lecia, that's it. I'll be at my parent's house. Where is your phone?"

"In my purse." I went inside her purse without permission, retrieved it, and I plugged in the dead phone to charge it.

"I'll call you in the morning."

"Ok, thanks for coming," she told me as if she were thanking an old friend for showing concern. I bowed my head, thankful she was at least talking to me, and kissed her on the cheek again, then tenderly rubbed her hand, which was placed on the top of her belly.

"Bye Lecia, I love you."

"Bye Cade, we'll be fine." She massaged her swollen belly and turned her attention back to her father, then pulled her chair closer to the bed before I could give one last kiss to my son. I turned one last time to look at her before leaving the room.

It was late when I arrived at my parents' home. No one was waiting up for me and I let out a sigh of relief that I was able to make it to my room to get some sleep without an interrogation from my family. I took off my clothes and jumped in bed, knowing I would have a better chance of convincing Lecia to return home once we both got some rest.

Morning came early, and I didn't get up soon enough to allow an escape from my parents' questions or their demands for answers that I knew awaited me. I washed and put on some clothes and went to the kitchen, where my mother was cooking, and greeted her with a kiss.

"Good Morning Cade. Is Lecia still in bed resting?" She was busy fussing over the contents simmering in the pan on the stove.

"No Mom. She was at the hospital with her father when I got here last night, and she wanted to stay with him." I didn't have too long to wonder if my mother knew what had happened between us since my mother and Dana were close and she'd probably told her about the state of my marriage. My mother continued the discussion as I held my breath, uncertain of how I was going to explain the situation between me and Lecia.

"Marisela called to let me know about Aridio. I'm sorry to hear about his accident." She kept her back to me as she spoke.

"Yes, it has us all worried. So, Dana hasn't said anything about Lecia?" I threw my question out there and looked at her. If we needed to get things out in the open, now was a good time.

"No Cade. Is there something else I should know?" She turned and looked back at me, her head cocked to the side.

"Mom, it's complicated between me and Lecia right now. You just need to know that she won't be staying here while she's in Charlotte."

"What's complicated about where she stays? She has always spent at least one night here with the family. Are the two of you arguing? Kaiden Moore, you know that strain in your relationship can't be good for Lecia or the baby."

Here we go again, bad, bad Kaiden. Somebody else worried about the baby. My brain was screaming in protest: *Don't say it. Pass on that comment,* but I couldn't restrain myself.

"What about me Mom? What about my needs as a man and a musician?" My father came into the kitchen and I stood while he gave me his quick, manly embrace.

"Good morning son. Glad you're back home." He provided a needed break in the tension growing between me and my mother. The respite was brief.

"What about you Kaiden? Are you asking me, what about you?"

The tone in her voice was becoming terser as the volume of her voice increased. My mother was one of the most compassionate people I knew; she rarely judged me and had always supported me throughout my life, but don't mess with her relationship with her grandchildren, even if the one in question hadn't been born yet.

"Cade, you know I love you, but you're surprising me right now. Have you really become the self-absorbed musician who only has room in his life for his art? Your father-in-law is fighting for his life, your wife is worried about her father, the health of your unborn child may be affected by the stress that Lecia is under, and you ask me, what about you?" She brought the pan of eggs over to the table and emptied some of it on my father's plate.

I should have taken another pass and stayed on the high road, but my response again was not wise, nor in my best interest.

"Mom, it's not my fault what happened to Lecia's father, and maybe I'm not Vincent who thinks that fatherhood is the best thing that ever happened to him. I don't know if I'm ready to be a father. Everyone can't be like your perfect firstborn son."

Vincent and Dana came into the kitchen just as I finished spilling my guts. My father still hadn't weighed in on the volley of comments between me and my mother, and I had definitely hit a nerve with her. I didn't know how much Vincent and Dana heard before they entered, and he seemed preoccupied listening to something Dana whispered in his ear before she left the room. I turned back and awaited my mother's response. Her face was reddened with anger and her lips were drawn tight.

"Cade, it's about time you resolve this issue you've had with your brother all of your life. I'm telling you, it's time you crawl out of your brother's shadow and stop the comparisons that exist mainly in your mind. Are you so concerned you'll have to give up your music if you become a father and then what will you have? My goodness, what would you fall back on? Whatever will you have in your life that makes you feel you're just as good as your brother?" She was throwing out sarcasm, cooking it and sliming me with it at the same time. She placed a plate of eggs and bacon in front of me. I loved her eggs, but my appetite was gone.

"I'll no longer accept responsibility that maybe your father and I did something to make you feel not as good as your brother. I know you love Vincent and you're aware he loves you and would do anything for you. You tell me all the time that he's your best friend. This competition thing you have with him has to stop."

I felt the full weight of shame and looked at Vincent, who kept his eyes on his hands in his lap. My mother hadn't finished sharing a piece of her mind with me yet and we, as the men in the family, knew to remain quiet and let her find her peace.

"And, by the way, it's too late to wonder about fatherhood. I don't know if you recall, but you've got a pregnant wife. Man up son. It's time."

This time I didn't have it in me to respond. I knew I'd had this coming for quite some time, and my father at first sat quietly but after listening to the whirl of the ceiling fan, the only sound in the room for a few minutes, he chose to enter the conversation.

"It's not you or Cade who's to blame Lauren, it's me." We were all sitting at the table and looked up at him, not sure where he was going with this.

"Cade is acting just like I once acted when I felt cornered. It took me a long time to reflect on my behavior, but I realized I'd allowed the distance to grow between you and me early in our marriage because I felt pushed aside by our first pregnancy and the family's response to our baby.

There was always someone around, and I was wrong to feel that you no longer had time for me. I shared my experiences with Vincent when Dana got pregnant for the first time. He prepared for it and was a better man than me when Alex came along. Cade needed his space too and he's not wrong for it. We've always provided him with space for his music and he needs the space for his creativity to flourish. I wanted it to be a surprise for him and Lecia, but I purchased the vacant apartment next to their apartment from the Turlingtons and Vincent agreed to design the space that they'll need for their growing family after we knock out the walls."

"Surprise," Vincent said with guilt written on his face.

"Try not to be too hard on him Lauren. I know you're afraid that you may not have a close relationship with his child if the problems between him and Lecia worsen. We can only pray that they'll find a way to work out their differences. Having a little more space at home should help, and I hope you two weren't too disturbed by the noise."

"Thanks Dad, that was very thoughtful of you and we were dealing with the noise." I humbly looked at my parents and got up to first embrace my mother, then my father, because I knew she wanted what was best for me and my family.

"Thanks bro. We'll talk more about this later." I punched Vincent on the shoulder before turning back to face my mother.

"Mom, you know how much I love Lecia, and we're going through a rough patch that is largely my fault, but there's nothing I wouldn't do to let Lecia know how much I want her and my baby." I sat back down and choked on the lump in my throat.

"I know son, and you know we're rooting for the two of you, but in the meantime let's eat something."

We managed to get through our breakfast in silence, and each bite was painful to swallow as I thought about the state of my marriage.

Holding my head down to hide the fear in my eyes, I didn't see when Dana entered the room with Lecia in tow. She was standing in the doorway of the kitchen when I looked up and saw her sad brown eyes resting on me. She looked tired—as if she hadn't slept in days.

"Lecia, what's wrong? Did something else happen to Aridio?"

She burst out crying before she could answer my questions, and I got out of my chair, racing to take her into my arms and comfort her.

"Tell me what's wrong." I tried to encourage her to speak to me as I led her to the window seat, so we could sit side by side. She didn't resist coming into my arms and continued to drop silent tears while I comforted her. My family members were observing us while trying to pretend they were more interested in eating their breakfast. She finally spoke to me.

"Cade, the baby stopped moving and he hasn't moved at all today. I'm worried something is wrong. I don't want to burden you, but I don't want to lose my baby."

She started crying again, and I thought it best to ignore her reference to our child as her baby. I wiped away her tears and, placing my hand on her belly, I did what came naturally to me.

"Boy, why are you worrying your mother? Are you tired too?"

I didn't know if we were having a boy, but in that moment, it just felt right to call the baby my boy. We were comforting each other just as we always had despite our differences. What was different this time was we were connecting with each other for the first time in a while. She smoothed my hair and kissed the top of my head as I leaned in and planted kisses on her belly.

"There's nothing wrong with our boy." In that same moment I saw the slow wave of Lecia's belly moving under my hand. She placed her hands, on top of mine and my mother, now seated at the table and the closest to us, began tearing up.

"Our son was missing his daddy." Lecia was startled by his sudden movement and opened her mouth to smile as he kicked her hard inside her belly.

"Lecia, please come and rest with me. I promise I won't pressure you to stay after you wake up from a nap."

"You don't have to pressure me Cade. I'll stay with you if that's what it takes to keep the baby active and moving. I don't want anything to happen to my baby because I haven't been careful with my health. We both need you."

"I need you and I'm asking for your forgiveness. I know I haven't handled things well, but you know I love you and *our* son. I want us to stay together as a family."

"We both did things that we couldn't see at the time that could've been perceived as insensitive, and we both could benefit from forgiving each other."

We were talking to each other as if we weren't being observed by others, but she was familiar with the dynamics of the Moore family. She was now a Moore and had grown comfortable with having the hard conversations in front of the family when we had to. She knew my family loved her very much and would do anything to support the stability of the family we were creating. I took her into my lap and kissed her on the lips but stopped myself before I took her tongue into my mouth in a manner not appropriate for a morning breakfast with my parents.

"Babe let me take you back to our room, so you can get some rest."

"That sounds like a good idea. I'm exhausted." Here was where she belonged, and thank goodness my son, my trustworthy ally, had reminded us both we belonged together no matter the circumstances that threatened to come between us.

"If y'all will excuse us, we're going back to bed." I helped Lecia to her feet.

"I'm sorry I didn't say hello to everyone as I entered the room, but I'm so exhausted and I was worried about the baby." Lecia went to the table and hugged my parents.

"No problem…it's alright…take care of yourself. We'll talk after you get some rest."

There was a litany of support as we excused ourselves and I guided her with reverence to our bedroom. She was the most precious thing in my world, my divine gift, and I planned to show her how much her forgiveness meant to me.

"I love you and the baby so much Lecia." Her love for me was pure, and she had always made me a better man. I assisted her in taking off her clothes and shoes and took her in my arms in a close embrace.

"I love you Cade, and I could never stop loving you. You don't have to worry about anyone coming between us." She was very tired, and her eyes were becoming heavily lidded as I helped her into bed. In the haze of fatigue, she looked into my eyes and asked me a question with an overlay of melancholy in her voice. "Cade, do you want to be a father to our child? I love you too much to ask you to do something you're not ready to do."

Pulling her chin up toward me and stroking it with tenderness, I didn't break the eye contact between us. I wanted her to look deep into my orbs, into the depths of my soul as I spoke, eye to eye, and closely pressed together, with one beating heart merged with the other. Her face relaxed as she read my true intent, and I felt she understood, that what I was about to say was the truth.

"I've always wanted a family with you. I love you and I love our child. I want my baby and no man will ever have the privilege of raising my son." I tried to hold back the bile rising in my throat as I thought about Marco's suggestion. "I had problems with all the baby stuff that kept appearing in our place. I was suffocating in the clutter and it seemed to make you happy, so I tolerated it at first, but I just couldn't do it anymore. I'm telling you I love you and this baby with all my heart and I'll be the best father I can be to my son. It just took me a while to realize it but it's the truth."

She looked at me and wiped away the tears forming in my eyes before giving me a heart-stopping kiss. My breath hitched as she took her lips off mine and told me her thoughts.

"I believe you'll make a great father, my sweet Cade." She nestled in my arms as I held her.

"Thanks for saving me from a family feeding frenzy. You showed up just when I needed you most. I love you so much." I kissed the top of her head.

"Dana told me you were probably going to get it and to get my ass over here. I was planning on calling you to tell you about the baby. I love you so much Cade, and I couldn't stop loving you in this lifetime or the next if I tried." She yawned and struggled to get out her words.

"I won't ever give you a reason to stop loving me." She fell asleep before I could tell her the plans for the apartment in New York. I settled in to rest alongside her, content my world was turning on a happier axis. I didn't believe it possible for me to feel so much fear and sadness, but I'd been on the verge of tears more in the past three days than in my entire adult life. I guess we were both hormonal.

Several hours later I returned to my parents' home from the recording studio I rented in downtown Charlotte. Lecia had been asleep when I'd snuck out without waking her, and I stopped by the hospital for a brief visit to check on Marisela and Aridio before returning home. Mom was in the family room talking to Dana.

"Hi Cade. How did it go today?" She was cheery. I guess I was back in her good graces.

"Hi Mom. Things were good, and we finished recording a track for the new album. I stopped by and saw Aridio today and he was stable." I gave them both a hug.

"Hey Dana, Lecia told me you called her, and I owe you one, Sis."

"No problem. That's what family's for."

My mom rubbed the back of her neck as she spoke to me. "Lecia told us about her visit with her father. She came back here after a few hours at the hospital and has been asleep for the last five hours. I checked on her earlier and I'm concerned she hasn't eaten much all day."

"I'll try to get her up to eat something, but she's so tired she may want to stay in bed and get some rest." I grabbed a few apple slices from on the counter and chewed them with delight.

"I love the fresh fruits down here. The apples are one of my favorites."

"I have plenty. Help yourself, but after you finish snacking, if you can convince Lecia to eat, I'll have something prepared for her."

"I'll go check on her now Mom."

I went to the bedroom and Lecia was still curled up under the plush bedding. I had to strain my vision to find her under the mounds of the thick white linen duvet. I peeled back the covers and her thick, curly hair was sprawled across the pillows. She moaned and protested as I delivered kisses on her face, neck, and breasts. Stirring a little more under my touch, she tried to reach for the covers to pull them back around her, but eventually she opened her eyes when I began talking about her Papi.

"I saw your parents today and Papi was still stable."

"Thanks for checking on them Cade. Mami made me leave to get some more rest since there were no changes in Papi's condition."

"She's right. You need to take care of yourself and I'm going to help you get in the shower and then we need to get something to eat."

"Do I stink?" She sniffed the air and I laughed at her.

"No, but a nice luxuriously warm shower will be good for you and the baby. You know, to help you relax." I helped her out of bed and into the bathroom, where I turned on the water while she undressed.

"I need to return a few calls and I'll be right back." I kissed her on the lips and on her round belly, which answered my touch with writhing movements.

"I'll be showered and dressed by the time you come back," she promised as I left her to enjoy a warm, relaxing shower. It took me about fifteen minutes to walk to the study and talk to my manager and members of the band before returning to the bedroom.

To my surprise, I returned and discovered she had gotten back in bed and was fast asleep. I peeled back the covers and revealed a naked Lecia with the serene look of a Madonna with child and her round belly thumping and calling out to be kissed. I lowered my head to kiss my son and touched both sides of her belly with my large hands. She stirred a little and I saw a smile spread across her face as I took in the smell of lavender on her skin.

"Wake up sleepy girl." I placed a trail of kisses on her lips and alongside her jaw, then sucked her protruding nipples, which puckered under my touch, and kissed under her belly as I turned her on her back. She smiled, still under the haze of sleep, as I pulled my shirt over my head, then pulled her legs apart and positioned myself between them. I bore my weight on my elbows, lowered my head between her legs and began tickling her with my tongue in between murmuring sweetly to her to lure her out of her dreamy state.

"I love you so much. You're so beautiful, my queen."

I didn't hold her down as her back arched, allowing closer contact between her pelvis and my head. Her eyes remained closed and her head turned from side to side as she moaned under my touch.

"Come on Lecia. Time to wake up, my love. I really need to feed you but first I'm going to eat you."

I lowered my head again and ran my tongue along the length of her inner thighs and up to her warm private lips, pouting for my attention. While I pulled on her bud, she mewed and moaned in response to her pleasure as I smiled in appreciation of the view of her private, inner sanctuary.

"Open your eyes babe," I commanded before touching her sweet spot and sending her over the edge as I had done many times before. Her slick walls contracted against my fingers and her breaths, which were now heavy pants, became less labored as she recovered from her orgasm. She had a moist sheen on her beautiful coffee with cream-colored skin, and her hair was wet against her face. To me, she was the perfect portrait of a sensual African-diaspora goddess with child. I could have beheld her beauty for hours, but I had to accomplish my task to get her fed, and I knew it wouldn't be much longer before someone came knocking on the door if we stayed in bed much longer.

"Lecia, baby, you can't go back to sleep. You haven't eaten much all day, so let me help you put on some clothes." I kissed her on the lips, so she could taste herself flavored with the smell of lavender from her body wash both still on my lips. She opened her eyes and began talking to me in a sultry voice.

"It's your turn, Cade. We're not finished." She looked at me with lidded sensual eyes.

"Not now baby." I pulled her up to a seated position before going to the closet to get a dress for her. "I'm serious babe, you've got to eat something."

"OK, OK. I'll cooperate." I was finally able to get some clothes on her before we left the room and walked hand in hand to the kitchen, where my mother and Dana were seated at the table. They greeted us as we entered the room, and I pulled out a chair for Lecia to have a seat with them at the table. My mother got up and placed a hot steaming bowl of chili in front of us. Lecia lowered her head and took a whiff of the smells coming from it.

"Mom is this mild turkey chili?"

"Yes, Marisela told me you were eating a lot of turkey chili before your father's accident. I thought it would be just the thing to get you to eat. I have butter pecan ice cream for your dessert—one of your favorites."

"Yum, Thank you. You're so kind." She rubbed her belly.

Lecia took the spoon from my mother, and I asked for a spoon to taste the chili.

"Cade, I can get you a bowl of your own. This is for Lecia."

"Mom, I just want to taste it."

She brought me a spoon and placed more chili in Lecia's bowl after she ate several spoons of the steaming mixture. The bowl, which was half filled with food, was refilled to the brim, and Lecia tilted her head back after she looked at the extra food in front of her.

"This is good Lauren, but I can't eat another bite." She placed her spoon back on the table beside her bowl while I lifted more chili to her mouth. She frowned but ate a little more.

"We have to feed my baby Lecia. Can you take in a little more?" I rewarded her with a kiss and a smile every time she tried to eat another spoon full of food.

"No more Cade; I'm full." She leaned in to rest her head against my chest.

"I need to go back to see my father, but truthfully, I'm so tired." She closed her eyes and stayed pressed against me.

"It's late. Let's stay here for now and we can go to the hospital together in the morning."

"Okay Cade, but I want to get there early."

"I promise we'll get there early."

"Did you sleep well my dear?" Lecia lifted her head from my chest and answered my mom with a stretch of her limbs and a covered yawn.

"I haven't slept that well since before my pregnancy. Where did you get the bed linens? They're so plush and heavenly."

"I ordered them just for you. I remembered how uncomfortable a protruding belly can be on your back. The mattress and bedding are part of the Resort collection and the linens are an Egyptian cotton sateen woven blend. I'm glad you're getting some rest, but we need to work on your appetite to keep up your strength."

"Good morning family." My sister, Doris Moore, came walking into the kitchen to the surprise of everyone. Doris was younger than Vincent but older than me and she was an acclaimed opera singer with a worldwide following. With more than a flair for the dramatic than Vincent and I could ever muster combined, she sauntered into the room like a model on a runway dressed in a red dress with a high split on the side. I wasn't sure when she started keeping her sunglasses on inside the house, but she kept them on until after she said her hellos.

"Hello dear. You didn't tell me you were planning to come home!"

"I'm a woman of mystery and surprises, Mom." She started with my mother and made her way around the table, sharing hugs and kisses. As was our custom, all conversations and attention shifted to her. She carried a box wrapped in paper covered with little blue bunnies that looked like a present for a baby shower or a gift for a newborn.

"Hi Dana."

"Hi Doris." She embraced and kissed me and Lecia on both cheeks, a habit she had grown accustomed to after her extended stay on a European tour. We returned her greeting and watched her with our full attention broken only by the smells of her expensive perfume.

"What scent are you wearing? It smells so good." Lecia took in the scent still wafting in the air while Dana and my mother nodded.

"I can't remember the name of it, but I'll send you all a bottle. Cade do you want some too?" She pulled out a chair and took a seat.

"I think I'll pass but thanks."

"Suit yourself." She held her palm in the air in an affected manner.

"Y'all know I've been staying at Vincent and Dana's place in New York before my next upcoming performance since my apartment is still being remodeled and the delays have been tiring. Anyway, I decided on a whim to come home after I heard what happened to Mr. Tavares. I probably won't get to see you again, Lecia, before you deliver, so I brought this present to give to you in person."

Doris placed the present in Lecia's lap and began singing a sweet melody with her head leaned in just above Lecia's belly.

"Hello, my sweet baby," Doris sang. Lecia smiled after I placed my hand on her belly, which tightened then relaxed in waves moving across her abdomen.

"Is the baby giving me applause?"

"He enjoys when he hears someone singing. Cade sings to him often and he likes when his daddy lays his strong hand on my belly. The baby always seems to move in the direction of the pressure from Cade's hands."

"That's interesting but let me get back to telling you something that was kind of strange. I received an unexpected visit from a woman dressed in medical scrubs named Tessa Mann. She told me she knew you and she was just getting off from work and needed to deliver a present for Lecia and the baby. She had this odd story that one of Lecia's former colleagues wasn't welcomed at your home Lecia, so she, that being Tessa, agreed to deliver the package to Dana. I believe you all sweat it out together at the gym? I assumed she was delivering the present from your ex-best friend Darlene Evans." Lecia rolled her eyes and Doris shrugged her shoulder as she told us the story.

"Was the package ticking?" I snorted, took the present from Lecia, and tore into the paper while keeping my eyes on Lecia, who remained silent as I opened the present. Inside the package was another stuffed animal, a bear dressed in scrubs with a stethoscope around its neck.

"Something for charity? The kids at the local charity here in Charlotte that you and Aria have been supporting will like this." Lecia nodded. We both were too tired for drama from Darlene. My family was aware the two of them were close friends at one point, but Darlene's jealousy of our happiness had driven a wedge between them.

"Is this woman still crazy over you Cade?"

Leave it to Doris to address all the sticky subjects.

"Yes," Lecia answered, rolling her eyes.

"Doris!" My mother called out and folded her arms.

"Don't blame me, Mom. It's the curse of the Moore men. Women lose their minds over them and resort to stalking them and their family. I don't get it."

"I don't like it either, but I get it Doris," Lecia told her. "It's easy to see how she could develop fantasies about my handsome Cade." I placed my arms around her and lowered my eyes. *Awkward.* Dana rescued me with her welcomed diversionary comments.

"Vincent had his share of stalkers too. We still have restraining orders against some of them."

Mother surprised me and chimed in. She was usually more reserved in discussing such topics. "Charles Aiden had women who were delusional about his love for them. They told me things about him to try to turn me against him. Girls, we're blessed to have our husbands' love, and other women may resent that. We must rise to the challenge as strong women who not only know our husbands aren't perfect, but they are worth fighting for. Never forget our vows mean something to us and we'll fight for our families. Let there be divine help to change the hearts of anyone who tries to break our bonds." She looked at me and continued.

"We may love our men, but they know there are deal breakers and not to try our patience."

I squirmed under her gaze but was surmised she was trying to tell me and Lecia something about staying focused on what was important as she looked at both of us then looked away. I cleared my throat and spoke up.

"Thanks Mom for your advice to keep the lines of communication open and that there is nothing more important than family. You know better than anyone when to give me a swift kick in the butt." Lecia looked at me with a shy smile.

"Did I miss something?" Doris leaned forward and looked around the table.

"Stay out of this Doris. I was reminding Cade of family as a priority and I may have been a little harsh yesterday, but I needed to impress upon him that I love him, Lecia, and that baby she's carrying. They will always be welcomed in this home for as long as I have breath. Your children will be

Moores' and it is their birthright to be here where people will always love and support them. Your children, Vincent's children, and the children that Doris will have in the future are important to me and your father."

She choked up but composed herself and continued while Doris choked probably on the thought of having children.

"We've worked hard to ensure that they will always have a place in the world to call home even if they are angry with you all as their parents. We'll always be here to help and provide whatever they need to grow into healthy, happy adults."

Whew! She's calling me Cade again instead of Kaiden. I guess I'm forgiven. I shifted my weight and my opinions about my mother's position, knowing the sacrifices both my parents had made to ensure we had a place to call home.

My father ran a successful real estate business, and he built my mother the estate she wanted in the trendy suburbs to welcome and protect her family against any disappointment or blows in life. My mother loved having all her children around her and was a formidable adversary to any threat to the family. Lecia got up to hug her and she yielded into her embrace.

"I love you Lauren Moore. I hope I can be the mother to my child that you've been to your children. I see why they adore you." My mother blushed, embarrassed but also appreciative of Lecia's comments. Vincent and my father entered the kitchen and they were surprised to see Doris seated at the table. She rose to run into my father's arms before going to kiss Vincent.

"You two smell fishy," she told them and wrinkled her nose.

"We were out on the boat." The smell of fish gave Lecia slight dry heaves and she convulsed her shoulders and placed her hand over her mouth before I took her by the hand and moved away from Vincent.

"The smell of fish getting to you?" Vincent asked Lecia. "Dana would turn green when she was pregnant if I came home smelling like fish."

Lecia placed a hand over her mouth and ran from the room to prevent hurling in front of everyone. I made haste and said goodbye before running off behind her.

CHAPTER FIVE

Four days passed since Papi had slipped into a coma, and Lecia was still maintaining a vigil at the hospital, but I was more successful in getting her to eat something during the day and leave the hospital at night to sleep in a comfortable bed. We were waiting for the doctors to come in with their daily report when in walked Dana with the twins, Mitchell Austin and Marie Ariadne, affectionately known as Austin and Aria, the youngest of their four children. She stopped just before they reached the bed to speak to them.

"Remember what I told you. Stay near me and don't touch anything." Aria, as energetic as ever, bounced into the room before Dana could grab her by the hand to restrain her.

"Papi, Papi, I came to see you today."

She spoke to him as she struggled to get on the bed where he was lying under the covers. He had fewer tubes around his body and his vitals were stronger, but he still hadn't opened his eyes. I was at the bedside holding Lecia's hand on one side of the bed and her mother, Marisela, and her sister Marissa were on the other side of the bed.

Beep. Beep. The lights and sounds of the monitors marked time as we held our breaths and looked on while no one stopped Aria, a precocious child of three years, from climbing the railings onto the bed with her Papi. She scampered alongside his body, lying in a tight posture with his head on the pillow, and kissed him on the cheek. Papi wasn't her biological grandfather, but it hadn't stopped the two of them from forming a tight bond of love and adoration ever since he met my extended family for the first time a year ago.

"Hola, Uncle Cade and Tia Lecia."

She greeted us and then the others by the bedside.

"Hola, Abuela and Tia Marissa," she smiled at members of Lecia's family before placing her little arms around a quiet Papi, who remained still and unresponsive.

"I'm sorry for the intrusion, but the twins were insistent on seeing Mr. Tavares. I thought that it could possibly help him to have them talk to him."

She attempted to get Aria off the bed, but Marisela stopped her.

"Please, let her stay with him. It may do him some good to hear the voices of so many who love him."

Aria took it as permission to continue to spend time with her Papi and she stretched out alongside him and placed her little hand in his.

"Papi, I have on the green dress you like. I put it on just for you. See Papi? Wake up and look at me Papi. I had Mommy put ribbons in my hair just for you Papi."

She cocked her head to the side, waiting for him to look at her, and leaned in to kiss him again.

"Austin came to see you too. Look at him Papi."

She pointed at her twin brother, then placed her hand on his cheek, but he still didn't move. She was too young to understand why he wasn't listening to her and she began to cry as she looked down upon him. Before her mother could get up to comfort her, one of her tears dropped on his face and I didn't know if it is what I wanted to see, or if my eyes were playing tricks on me, but his eyelids started to flutter, and his lips were moving but no sound came from them.

"Keep talking to him Aria," I encouraged her. "Papi isn't feeling well, but he heard you."

"Te amo, Papi," my sweet niece told him. He opened his eyes with much effort and turned his head to the sound of the voice of his little angel. He moved his head and looked at us gathered around his bedside and, as if by a miracle, he started to speak.

"Don't cry, Aria. Te amo tambien," he whispered in a low, raspy voice.

Marisela, Marissa, Lecia and Dana stood up around the bed and began crying. He took his other hand and patted her little hand wrapped around his and smiled at her.

"Did I do something wrong, Uncle Cade? Why are y'all crying?" Aria asked. Besides Papi, I was the only adult in the room who wasn't letting their tears flow freely.

"No, my sweet girl. You did a very good thing. You and Austin were just what Papi needed."

Taking Aria off the bed and gathering Austin beside me, I pulled them both into my arms. Marisela had alerted the staff by using the call button on the bed railing and informed them that Aridio had awakened from his coma. Several doctors and nurses came into the room to examine him and ask what happened.

We moved away from the bed to a corner of the room to let the staff examine him while Marisela told them what happened.

"Mrs. Tavares, this is obviously a good sign. We're hopeful for his recovery, but he's not out of the woods yet." One of the doctors took her hand and patted it before departing the room with the team.

Dana gathered the children and allowed them to give their Papi final hugs before they got kisses and warm embraces from all the Tavares women. I took pictures of Aria and Austin before they departed, and I planned to give Aridio a picture of Aria in the green dress he liked so much.

The dress did match her bright green eyes. We told the children frequently that love conquered many things and that a hug and kiss could make it all better. I was glad they believed us, and I saw for myself just how true the statement was. I pledged that I would make sure my children knew about the power of love. Love conquers all things.

By the end of the week, Aridio had continued to show signs of progress. His right leg was still in a cast from the fracture after the fall, but his mental state was showing signs of improvement. He was now alert and responsive to those around him, and we were all elated when he was moved to a room outside of the critical care unit and onto the general ward.

I went to the hospital every day for almost two weeks after his admission to the hospital and was about to enter his room through a door that had been left ajar when I heard an unfamiliar voice. Marisela called the woman Lydia, and I seemed to recall Lecia telling me Lydia was the name of Marco's mother. My suspicions were validated by Lydia's next comment.

"Lecia, you know I always dreamed of you and Marco getting married and having a family together. Why didn't you show Marco how beautiful and attractive you were when the two of you were together? Every time we saw you, you had on oversized scrubs or something else unappealing."

I listened at the door out of view, but I was able to peer in and see Lecia flex her neck backwards, rubbing the back of it, while keeping her eyes closed. She waited a moment and opened them slowly to look toward her father for support. Their eyes met and still she said nothing.

"Kaiden Moore comes along, and you become an alluring sexpot," Lydia continued.

"You know your parents would have bought you attractive clothes if you'd asked them. I know you have your pride, but there was no shame in admitting you couldn't afford them. If you looked as attractive back then as you do now, Marco would have never strayed away from you. That baby you're carrying could have been Marco's baby and my grandchild."

I had heard enough and placed my hand on the door but stopped as Aridio raised his hand and pointed a finger at Lydia.

"Enough, Lydia!" He spoke to her in a low and weakened but determined voice. There was no mistaking his disdain for the conversation, and he waved his hand in the air to dismiss further talk and furrowed his brows, glaring at Lydia before placing his hand to his throat to stifle a cough. He struggled to be heard, but the frown on his face spoke volumes. Marisela went to his bedside and tried to prevent him from saying more, but he continued.

"Lecia has held her tongue and tolerated your comments out of respect to us as her parents, and to you as a family friend, so I'll speak for her. She was never betrothed to your son, as if we'd agreed to some arranged marriage. We like Marco and I loved your husband as a brother. We not only built our businesses together and imagined enjoying success together from our hard labor, but we promised to do all we could to help each other succeed. But I stress to you that none of my daughters were ever promised to any man, including your son. Lecia is happily married to Cade and they have pledged their love and faith to each other."

Lydia held her chin high and turned her attention away from him.

"They're expecting their first child—my first grandchild—and I don't want you upsetting Lecia with more fantasies of what could have been. We supported Lecia's choice to marry Cade, and we couldn't be happier for them. I'll not hear you speak of these things to Lecia ever again, and if you do, I'll consider it a personal insult to me and my family." He settled back in his bed and Marisela placed her hand on his shoulder to soothe him.

"Please Aridio, Lydia didn't mean any harm." Marisela added. "She knows Lecia is happily married to another man. She was just sharing her disappointment that she won't be having a grandchild anytime soon."

He looked away, still angry, but didn't resist Marisela fluffing his pillows to attempt to soothe him. I used the lull in the conversation as my cue to enter the room and pushed open the door, announcing my entrance as I walked in as if I had just arrived.

"Hello everybody." I went to the bedside and placed a kiss on Aridio's forehead.

"Feeling better?" He nodded.

It was good to know we had his blessing and approval. Aridio and I had come a long way in our relationship with each other, and a year ago he wouldn't have been so adamant in defending Lecia's decision to marry me. I embraced Marisela before I went to Lecia and gave her a kiss. She was sitting on the loveseat by herself near the bedside, with pillows stuffed behind her back, and she got up with some effort on swollen feet. She placed one hand on her belly and one behind her to inch out of the deep-seated couch as I extended my hand to help her on her feet and placed my arms around her.

Act I. The Seed on FIre

"Senora Lydia Rodriguez, I don't know if the two of you have been introduced, but this is my husband, Kaiden Moore."

"Please call me Cade." I extended my hand to the middle-aged woman with salt and peppered hair sitting near the bedside, with her lips drawn as if she had sucked on a sour lemon. I looked into her eyes and caught her outstretched hand in mine, giving her my most warm and expressive smile; my grandmother once told me I could win any woman over with my smile. She responded to me with a reciprocal friendly smile, and I felt comfortable knowing she no longer wondered how I had won over Lecia. I had seen her son Marco in action at our wedding reception, and it was clear to me he didn't know how to cherish a woman. What I knew about Lecia was she needed to feel she was appreciated and cherished. I motioned her back to her seat and sat in an embrace with her while the others in the room looked on.

Marisela and Lecia gave me the updates from Aridio's medical team, and Lecia stayed in my arms. She knew me more than anyone alive, so there was no doubt in my mind that she was fully aware my physical contact with her was to stake my claim and establish my position in her life with all those in the room, especially Senora Lydia. Lecia was mine. She had left her father's house and was cleaved to me. I looked down and her tummy was moving the fabric of her top from side to side. It was probably just a need to stretch his limbs, but I felt my son was also asserting his presence in his mother's life.

"Lecia, our son is moving." I placed my hand on her belly and she rolled her eyes at me. I saw Aridio's eyes light up the room. *I had their attention now.*

"It's a boy?" He leaned forward and looked at her belly moving beneath my hand.

"Yes, it's a boy. I had an ultrasound yesterday after I left you and it was confirmed. We're having a boy, but I thought Cade wanted to keep it a secret."

Marisela cupped her hands over her mouth in surprise and Lecia looked at me sideways. "It's a boy, Aridio. Oh, Lecia and Cade, I'm so happy."

She and Aridio embraced and looked at Lydia and repeated, "It's a boy?"

Lecia nodded and began laughing with her mother, who came and embraced us just as I was pointing at my watch to give Lecia the signal that we should be leaving to go home if we were going to get some rest.

"Now that I know you're having a boy, I'll know what to buy for the baby," Senora Lydia told Lecia.

"I thank you for your generosity, Senora Lydia, but we've received so many things already, we're planning to give some of the gifts to charity, of course, with the consent of the giver. Our friends know we support many charities for children and young mothers who may not be able to afford items for their child." I informed her and turned to help Lecia out of her seat.

"We need to be going so Lecia can get some rest. I can't speak from experience, but I imagine it's tiring carrying a baby around all day."

Marisela and Senora Lydia nodded in simpatico. I had scored some points with my last comment, but Lydia looked at us as if she still had more to say before we departed.

"If I bought you something, I would expect it to be for *your* child. I won't consent to my gift being given to a stranger," Lydia replied, and the lemon-faced look returned.

I took Lecia's hand and shot a look of agreement with Aridio. *I've had enough of Lydia Rodriguez.*

Act I. The Seed on FIre

"Thank you for thinking about us Senora Lydia. Lecia has had at least four baby showers and leave of absence celebrations with enough presents to fill two apartments. So many people love her and wanted to be a part of our blessed event and we'll need to have another child to use all the things she has been given." I chuckled.

"No time soon Cade. Let's get the first baby out of me before you start thinking about a second child." Lecia went to the bed to kiss her father, hugged her mother, and told Senora Lydia goodnight before we left together. I kept my hand at the small of her back to guide her to the door.

We were waiting for the elevator before she asked if I'd heard any of the conversation before I came into the room.

"I felt your presence before I saw you enter the room." She grabbed my hand.

"I heard enough." I looked up at the numbers lighting up on the elevator panel above our heads.

"I didn't want to upset Papi, and that's why I didn't challenge Senora Lydia's comments. I knew she still hasn't accepted Marco's childless marriage and divorce and I also knew her comments said more about her than about us. I hope you understand that my silence wasn't evidence that I agreed with her. She has always been opinionated and sometimes inappropriately so."

"Lecia, I hope you understand that I don't expect you to defend every silly thing that is said about us. I was more concerned that she was upsetting you." The elevator arrived and the door opened.

"Please know that she, nor her sons Marco or Mario, have the power to upset me," I reassured her, and I ushered her into the elevator to start our trip home. Her father was getting stronger and I was hoping Lecia would agree to go back to New York with me within the week.

The next day, Lecia planned to go to the hospital later in the afternoon for her visit, so I left her in bed asleep. We had agreed last night that I would spend the morning with her father and let her get a little more rest. She and her mother planned to stay home this morning while I assisted Aridio.

I arrived at the hospital and went to his room, curious that his bed was empty, and he was nowhere in sight.

"Mr. Moore, Mr. Tavares was taken to get some tests done. You can make yourself comfortable until he returns," one of the nurses informed me. I sighed in relief that he hadn't suffered a setback. I had some quiet time to sit until he returned, so I took a seat and looked around the beige room with tailored beige and cream curtains at the window. I hadn't given much thought to the personal effects around the sunny room before today. The usual flat-screen television, commercial hospital furniture, and medical equipment around the room reminded its occupant that this wasn't home, but I also saw pictures on his bedside table of a young Aridio playing a guitar, pictures of him smiling with the family, and the framed picture I had given him of Aria in her green dress and matching green ribbons in her hair. I noticed a vintage guitar sitting on a stand and went to pick it up, strumming the instrument to see if it was in tune. I was so focused on the warm, rich sounds coming from it, and didn't realize the sounds of the guitar could be heard outside of the room until some of the patients walking the halls began popping in and asked me to keep playing. A nurse came in rolling Aridio back to the room.

"Good morning Aridio." He looked at me with his guitar in my hand.

"Good morning Cade."

I stopped playing and placed the guitar back on the stand to help his attendant get him back in bed and looked over my shoulder at the group of patients who had returned to the door to ask me to play a few more songs. Aridio was in his bed and looked at those gathered in his room.

"Any requests?" I asked him, and he suggested that I play an old familiar Latin tune. I was grateful I knew how to play that song without sheet music since I had performed it at a local Latin-American festival years ago. He sat back, closed his eyes as I played, and a smile spread across his face. I ended the song and he opened his eyes to the sounds of the other patients clapping while standing with the help of walkers and canes. After the applause, they returned to their physical therapy of walking up and down the halls. Aridio waited until we were alone before he spoke.

"I never told you that, when I was a young man, I was a local musician in the Dominican Republic. I fell in love with Marisela, and her father wouldn't give me his blessing to marry her unless I got a *real* profession. My father had a construction company, and I agreed to stop playing gigs to work for him to win the hand of the woman I loved. I lost a part of my soul when I gave up my music. Life was fine after we got married and had children, but I lost my son Miguel, Lecia's twin brother, when they were three years old, and another part of me died. I knew I needed to leave the Dominican to start a new life and to find myself. I had to get away from all the ghosts of the past and make a new life for me and my young family. I've had a lot of time to think about things sitting in this bed, and the truth is, some of my anger toward you when I heard Lecia was falling in love with you wasn't just because you were a musician but because you were braver than I was, and I resented you because of your bravery. You held on to your passion for music, and I'd caved in because I was afraid Marisela would not have me without her father's approval. I didn't trust our love. You and Lecia trusted each other and you held on to your love for each other even when I made it difficult for you. I ask your forgiveness, Cade. I had no right to ask you to choose between love and your music. I guess I have to admit that I thought no man was good enough for my girl." I squirmed, reflecting on Aridio's confession as I pondered what to say.

"I appreciate and am thankful for you sharing your experiences with me, and I've always felt you just wanted the best for Lecia. I had to trust you would see that I was the right man for her. It also helped to finally hear that you didn't think Marco was that man." Aridio sat up taller in the bed.

"Marco and Mario have been indulged by their mother, and it has always concerned me, especially since the death of their father, that their mother's indulgence made Marco a man who thought he was entitled to anything and anyone he wanted. As for his older brother Mario, there has always been a darkness in his spirit I've never trusted. I don't believe he is an honest man, but Lecia doesn't see it. She thinks both Marco and Mario are misunderstood and that I haven't been fair in my judgment of Mario. Cade don't ever trust him."

"Thanks for the advice. There's something about Mario I don't trust either, but I can't put my finger on why I've always felt this way. He hasn't done anything to me, at least nothing I know about." I paused before I continued. "I came early today because I have to go back to New York to finish working on an album. Lecia will be staying here, but I hoped to convince her to come back to New York with me. I know she probably won't leave just yet, so I plan to commute until she's comfortable coming back home. The baby will be due soon, so we'll need to decide on either having him in New York or here in Charlotte." Aridio sat up and looked me in the eyes.

"I'm getting stronger every day. I'll need to continue my physical therapy to support the healing of my leg, but I want Lecia to focus on you and the baby. Not me."

"She thinks she can do both. You know how headstrong she can be."

"Yes, I think she got her stubborn streak from her mother."

He looked at me and smiled. I thought it better to let that thought hang in the air and not challenge the origins of one of Lecia's endearing traits. I spent the rest of the morning with Aridio, engaged in talk about music and sports and helped him with grooming and dressing. We received several requests to join the other patients after lunch in the gathering room.

The nurses were able to find another guitar for me to play, and Aridio played his guitar as the lead while I accompanied him, playing and singing backup. I set my phone on record to save our live recording, as I was amazed at his rich falsetto, which was growing stronger every day. His passion for Latin jazz still came through in his playing, and we played three songs to the applause of patients and staff.

Lecia, Marisela, and Marissa arrived on the ward and joined the others in clapping and shedding tears of joy. Lecia held her belly as she looked at me and her father enjoying the rousing applause.

"Papi has come a long way. Thank you for being there for us," she whispered in my ear.

"Yes, he has," I reflected. "We've all come a long way." I strummed the guitar one last time.

Michele Sims

CHAPTER SIX

Lecia was in her thirty-sixth week of pregnancy, and I had grown accustomed to the routine of commuting between Charlotte and New York. We finally made the decision to have the baby in New York with the delivery team and pediatrician at her place of employment. I was looking forward to my final trip to North Carolina to retrieve my family, as it would be our last planned trip to the South before Lecia gave birth.

Man, I was tired, but I would do it again if that was what I needed to do to keep the peace. Lecia had accepted that her father's condition had improved, and her mother didn't need her daily assistance. We spent one more night at my mother's insistence before going to Lecia's parents' house to say goodbye. My mother was at the stove finishing up a Southern breakfast of grits, sausage, bacon, pancakes, and a lighter fare of fruits and assorted pastries while Lecia sat nursing her cup of decaffeinated tea when my mother asked about the progress on our home.

"The walls have been knocked out and Vincent and his crew have been over every day placing the finishing touches on the remodeling project. There was so much dust from cutting the drywall and paint droppings, I had a moving team come and place most of our things in storage until next week." My mother was listening to me as my father entered the room and greeted us as he took a seat at the table.

"I'm sorry, I had them deliver the nursery furniture three weeks ago, but Lecia, I saw how long you looked at the complete ensemble that included the crib, changing table and rocker. Your eyes lit up with excitement when you saw that nursery set online, and you liked all the positive reviews, but your countenance fell when you scrolled down and saw the price. You left your laptop open, so I looked at it on the screen and I also fell in love with the set. I could tell it was the set you wanted but you weren't ready to settle on the price, so I bought it and had it shipped as a surprise to you. Your father had his accident and I just forgot I hadn't asked how it looked. Did you get a chance to set it up?"

Lecia looked up from her cup and stared first at my mother and then at me.

"Yes, we did. Dana and I hired some movers and they immediately went to work setting it up. Here, I have pictures of it." Lecia went to retrieve her purse and pulled out the pictures of the nursery. I tried to smile, but my memories weren't good ones of the night I came home and saw the nursery for the first time. My mother took the pictures and began smiling.

"Oh, Lecia. The room is lovely. My grandson will feel so loved and protected in his new room. You did a great job setting up the nursery." Lecia pushed her cup away from her and cocked her head to the side as she looked at me side-eyed, trying to read my face.

"Lauren, so you sent the nursery furniture without Cade knowing anything about it?"

"Yes dear, it was a surprise for both of you." This time it was my mother's turn to cock her head to the side, as if she wasn't sure of what was happening. Lecia turned her attention to me.

"So, Cade, you don't recall me telling you I was going to set up the nursery?"

"No, I don't recall." I rubbed the back of my neck and she turned to face me.

"You don't recall the night before you saw it, I kissed you after you came to bed and told you about it? You had a long set that night and I told you how happy I was to get the crib. I also told you I may have to put it in another room since it looked like it wasn't going to fit in the smaller room. I think it was three in the morning when we had that discussion and you said, 'Sure babe, whatever you think is best.'"

"Lecia, you know I don't remember most things when I get home that late, and I don't recall you talking about a nursery." It was about that time she leaned her head back and began laughing. She looked at me looking back at her, and tears began to fall she was laughing so hard. Dana and Vincent were home with the kids for the weekend and they walked into the room for an early morning breakfast before the kids got up.

"What's so funny?" Vincent asked as he and Dana looked on and laughed because of Lecia's infectious laughter, which went on for a few minutes.

"I'm not sure, but Lecia is laughing because of something about the nursery," I tried to explain. I was becoming concerned she couldn't stop laughing and that it may send her into labor, but she finally calmed down to explain.

"Lauren sent the crib—" more laughter. "Remember Dana we set up the nursery?" Her head was now on my shoulder as she convulsed in more laughter.

"We came home—" She stopped to wipe the tears from her eyes and then she stopped laughing.

"I thought he...he. Oh, never mind what I thought." There was a moment of silence followed by a torrent of tears.

I finally got it. It took a while, but the pain she was covering by first suppressing her feelings then by the volcanic eruption of nervous laughter had broken through.

"You thought I was upset because I saw the nursery and I couldn't hide it any longer that I didn't want the baby?"

Dana handed her a tissue and she nodded.

"You thought I was in on the surprise with my mother and since you told me you were setting up the nursery, it had to be something more than just the furniture in my room? Lecia, I didn't know or at least didn't remember that I was losing my composition room. I was tired and just didn't handle it well."

She nodded, acknowledging her painful thoughts and kept her face covered on my shoulder while she spoke.

"And I'm so ashamed I drove a wedge between you and your family by making them believe you didn't want the baby." I took her into my arms and began stroking her hair.

"There's nothing to be ashamed about, it was just an unfortunate misunderstanding." My mother, who was always good at smoothing over family conflicts, came over and pulled up a chair to take Lecia into her arms.

"Lecia, you know there are no wedges or walls between us in the Moore family. You know how we are. We can have spirited discussions, but at the end of the day, we're family. I may not like everything Vincent, Cade or Doris may do, but I realize I must respect their thoughts and opinions as adults just like I respect you and Dana. You have nothing to be ashamed of. You know Cade. You love him, and you know how much he loves you and that baby you're carrying. Dry your eyes, and in the future, we'll all laugh about this." I handed her a napkin from the table.

"Mom, you didn't see Cade's face when he opened the door and saw the crib and all his instruments gone." I looked at Vincent as my parents and his wife glared at him.

"Too soon?" He placed a piece of toast in his mouth and changed the subject.

"The renovations are on schedule and should be ready before Lecia returns home next week. That's the good news of it."

I stroked the length of her back, happy I could focus on more pleasant things. Lecia would be home next week, and my baby would soon be here. She took a breath and leaned up out of my mother's embrace.

"When does this hormonal stuff end?" she asked. "I'm an emotional chameleon, laughing hysterically one moment and in tears the next."

We left my parents' home and went to Aridio and Marisela's home on our way to completing the Goodbye North Carolina tour, for now. Lecia was in her parents' room helping her mother with a few chores while Aridio completed his physical therapy session at home, and I was in the kitchen returning a few messages when Lecia's cousin, Antonio Tavares, came in the house through the side door. He stopped when he saw me sitting at the table.

"Hello, Cade. I didn't know you were back from New York. How long are you staying?"

I cocked an eyebrow at him and took my time to respond. He choked on the orange juice he had poured into his glass from the carafe, which sat surrounded by ice, in a bowl on the table.

"Trying to get rid of me already?" I knew he was friends with the Rodriguez brothers.

"Hey, I didn't mean anything by it. I just didn't know you were coming back so soon. Are you and Lecia staying here?"

"No, actually we're leaving later today." He gulped down the remainder of his juice and rubbed his tongue across his lips to catch the last sweet drop of juice. He tightened his lips and seemed to be struggling with the idea of saying more to me. I looked away from my phone and placed it on the table. Antonio was Lecia's younger cousin, and she told me he was a good guy but lacked focus and a father figure in his life.

"Cade, you know despite what my uncle used to say about you and some of the things the Rodriguez homies still say about you, you're one of the good guys. I've never seen anyone win over Aridio Tavares outside of some of our family members in such a short period of time as you have. I know he respects you—a lot. Did you hear how he fell from the ladder?"

"No, I just heard he had an accident."

"An avoidable accident, but I don't think he remembers all the details. At first, I thought I was off the hook because he couldn't remember, but my conscience is beating the hell out of me. I don't sleep most nights and I need to confess something. Can I tell you the truth?"

Why me and why now?

"Antonio, I'm not a priest and I have my own share of shortcomings. Don't you think you should talk to someone else, maybe a spiritual leader if you have need of confession?"

"No, you're close enough, and besides, you are family and you know how to keep your mouth shut. I could tell you

didn't tell Lecia about the money you loaned me last month."
I turned to face him and gave him my attention.

"I was at the bottom of the ladder holding it for Tio
Aridio when Mario came over and demanded I come to the
car to talk to him. He wanted to make sure I didn't tell Tio
he was stealing money from his mother and, by extension,
my tio since Aridio often covered the shortfalls of their
monthly expenses. Mario's father and Tio were close, and
some say during their youth, thick as thieves. Mario had
given me one thousand dollars a month ago, he said with no
strings attached, but he later told me it was stolen money and
my tio would never believe I didn't help him steal it. That's
why I came to you to ask for a loan. I needed to give Mario
the money back. I don't want anything more to do with him,
and I wanted to warn you about him. He's bad news, amigo.
I guess Tio got tired of waiting for me to return and tried to
climb down the ladder, but it gave way and he fell. I heard
the crash and ran to the back of the house while Mario sped
away. He didn't even stay to help me, and I called for help
when I discovered him on the ground."

I rubbed my cheek and closed my eyes. *Confession may
be good for the soul, but now what am I going to do with this
mess slimed all over me?* I couldn't keep this from Lecia
indefinitely, but I didn't want to upset her so close to
delivery.

"Antonio, I think you may be underestimating your
uncle's ability to forgive your errors in judgment. You may
decide to keep it from him; your choice. But can you live
with a lie? You've already said your conscience is whipping
up on you. I'll promise to hold my tongue and not involve
Lecia before the baby comes, but I can't promise anything
after that. She's been looking over her father's books, and
I'm sure she'll run across financial discrepancies if she

hasn't already done so. Thanks for the warning about Mario, but let me ask you something? Why do you think Lecia can't see the truth about either Mario or Marco?"

"I think, Cade, it's because Marco is deep down a good guy, but his brother has always been a bad influence on him. Lecia and Marco grew up together, and for most of their lives they acted more like brother and sister than girlfriend and boyfriend, but that changed after the death of Senor Rodriguez. Mario came home for the funeral from out west and never left. He convinced Marco that Lecia was fine and he should hit that thing."

My back stiffened as I listened to my wife's virtue being reduced to a thing.

"Sorry hermano, but you know my cousin is fine. She's beautiful inside and out, although I don't think she realizes she's hot." I grew impatient and furrowed my brow. Antonio cleared his throat and continued.

"My cousin had many suitors, but Mario convinced Marco to pursue her as a love interest, which I think killed their relationship. Marco was all macho, and he wanted them to have a sexual relationship. Lecia loved Marco, but she was never in love with him, and she wasn't interested in taking the relationship to another level, so Marco cheated on her and he found himself trapped in a marriage with a women he once lusted for. Lecia blamed herself for Marco's trouble and became a sympathetic ear as he went through a nasty divorce. Now he wants to get back with her, but I know that will never happen. She's crazy in love with you."

"We love each other, and I don't think even death will change that. So, was that so hard telling me the truth?"

"No, it wasn't so bad."

"I try to live a life free of secrets so I'm free to think about my future in a positive light and dream of pleasant things. I'm obsessed with my wife, and our love is on the top of my list of favorite things. I see her in rhymes and melodies and her name is a song to me and the music of my life. Free yourself Antonio, so that you may pursue pleasant things. I won't keep secrets from her. Lecia is too important to me and she's my every heartbeat. Secrets and lies between people are the death of the soul in any relationship."

"Did I hear my name called?" Lecia walked into the kitchen and gave me a kiss.

"I was just telling Antonio how important a life filled with love and truth is."

"That's an interesting poetic conversation for the two of you. I wasn't aware the two of you talked of such things."

"Unexpected circumstances change people and their relationships with each other." Antonio nodded in agreement.

"If you say so. I came to tell you I needed to take a nap before our flight back home tonight. Will you be okay while I lie down?"

"I can get some work done while you rest babe."

"Good," she was about leave when Antonio stopped her.

"Prima, I'm leaving to check on a job site after I speak to the folks. I hope the two of you have a safe trip back to New York."

He hugged Lecia and gave me our customary male handshake before leaving to find Marisela and Aridio. I was just about to get up to escort Lecia to her bedroom when the door opened, and it was Marco who came in and smiled at Lecia before he saw me sitting at the table.

"I think I'll take that nap later. Come on in Marco and have a seat. Did you come to visit with Papi?" Lecia looked warily between the two of us staring at each other.

Michele Sims

CHAPTER SEVEN

"What you got to drink? That's okay. Don't mind me, I know Marisela has some of her berry flavored tea in the fridge for me. She keeps the things I like around the house just in case I stop by for a visit. By the way, where is she and Aridio?"

"Mami is in her room rearranging things for Papi. I helped her move a few chairs so Papi could move his wheelchair around the room without bumping into things at every turn."

Marco went to the refrigerator and stood in front of the open door, bent at the waist, looking inside for so long, the cool air condensed on the side of the door into little droplets and ran down the side of the white rubber insulation encasing the inside of the door. He finally drew a pitcher containing a dark raspberry tea off the shelf and proceeded to the cabinet to get a glass. Again, he took his time moving glasses around, looking for a specific one. "Here it is. My favorite glass."

There was nothing special about the blue colored cut glass. I had seen several of them, but if it was his favorite, so be it. Lecia looked at me and squirmed in her seat as she extended her neck and cupped the back of it to rub away the tightness. She often did that to relieve stress.

First Lydia and now Marco. Keep it together Moore. You know Marco is trying to play you.

The chair scraped across the floor as I pulled away from the table with just enough room to cross my leg and place my hands behind my head.

83

Might as well enjoy the show.

"I didn't know you were planning to come back so soon Cade. Lecia told me you were working on a little project." Lecia was about to pipe in, but Marco gulped down his tea and poured himself another glass.

"This is so good, and I've often told Marisela her tea is the nectar of the gods. I don't know why she won't share the recipe with Mami. She shooed me out of the kitchen the last time and told me I always had a way with words. Why didn't you call me to help you move things? I was available."

"Cade's last project won him and his band numerous awards, and his current project is a much-anticipated album to capitalize on his recent successes. His band Fortune is almost finished with the recording of the album." She smiled at me and patted my leg.

"Then what? On the road to leave you alone to care for the new baby?" He laughed out loud, and if Lecia blinked any more, I'm sure her brain would have started to convulse in seizures.

Stay cool, it's wiser to avoid taking the bait. He's such a fool.

"Speaking of babies, my mother told me she finally met you, Cade, and how *charming* you are. I have to give you credit. You won the heart of the princess and left me to deal with my mother, who's still grieving over a grandchild she has never had. It was fine when she and Marisela didn't have grandchildren, but now that you two have one on the way, that's the only thing she talks about. Mario doesn't come around as much because he's sick of hearing what we haven't done with our lives."

What does that have to do with us? I focused on avoiding the eye roll.

"We don't measure up to men like the Cade Moores of the world, but I told her, Lecia, you and I have history and we'll always have history. Remember when I used to pick you up at night after your babysitting jobs? It was me who made sure you got home safely. Did Lecia tell you our families have known one another since before we emigrated from the Dominican Republic to North Carolina? We have history and I know people in our community who thought we would marry one day. And—"

My heart was beating so hard listening to this jackass, I was surprised it wasn't heaving my chest and snapping the buttons on my shirt. I narrowed my eyes and measured my words. I wanted no mistake in what I was about to say, and I planned to say it only once. I uncrossed my leg and leaned forward.

"Marco, I understand you and Lecia have history, but Aridio made it clear to me he never intended to see the day when you married Lecia. I don't want to speak for her, but it's my understanding she loved you as any dear friend would love another, but she was never *in* love with you. I hope you'll understand me being forthright with you, but you've been nothing but direct with me. I've been a man who has always spoken his mind and I find it refreshing to discover the same thing in you, so let me be clear. How often you come here to visit Aridio and Marisela isn't my concern, but I hope you'll respect my home and limit your calls to Lecia as she will be busy taking care of our son." His back stiffened and he had the same sour look on his face he must have inherited from his mother.

I looked at Lecia for the first time since Marco began his little show and waited for the answer. "Lecia, do you have a problem with me speaking my mind?"

"No, and I'm sure Marco doesn't mind you being honest with him if you give it to him with respect."

"Yes, we can respect each other as men." Marco added.

"Sounds reasonable, so let me finish and I'll be as brief as possible. The trips down memory lane and the calls to talk about your problems must come to an end. Lecia has a heart of gold, but she's not your therapist, and guilting her into listening to you about your mother's lack of a grandchild isn't our problem. I need to draw some lines as the man of my household. It's not a jealousy thing, but as a real man, I'm sure you understand my position."

Marco said nothing but looked at me as if I had just kicked sand in his face and thrown his lollipop in the sand. Marisela came in the door and looked at all of us seated at the table. The air was charged as Marco and I looked at each other.

"Is everything alright?"

"Yes Mami, everything is fine. Marco was visiting with us and enjoying a glass of your tea." She smiled at all of us, then went to the cabinet to get a glass and filled it with tea.

"Marco, I'm glad you're here. You can help me move a few things around while you visit with Aridio. Lecia, why don't you take Cade to the music room Aridio is trying to set up. He wanted some advice from Cade before you leave. I haven't seen him this excited in a long time, and he's already looking forward to the next, how you say, jam session between the two of you."

"Sure Marisela, I'll be happy to offer some advice."

"Come on Marco. I have a few things for you to do." He got up from the table and followed Marisela without looking back.

"Angry with me Lecia?" I needed to know her feelings.

"No, you were respectful." She kissed me on the lips and stroked the side of my face. "I enjoyed seeing in-charge Cade." Another kiss landed sweetly on my lips. "My no-nonsense Cade," followed by a third kiss. "My husband Cade, who is very secure in my love for him. My Cade who has no room for jealousy." I closed my eyes and waited for more kisses, but no warmth touched my lips, so I opened my eyes and stuck out my lips in disappointment.

"What? No more kisses?" I leaned in for more.

"Follow me, I'll need to give you a reward in private."

I straightened the bulge in my pants and followed her to our bedroom at the opposite end of the house.

We had a smooth flight back to New York and arrived back home late at night. A blue satin ribbon had been placed across the door and tied into a bow outside of our apartment. Lecia looked at me and cupped her mouth in surprise.

"What have you done?"

"We're not going to have another misunderstanding, so I'll admit I don't know what's going on. I'll wager a guess that Dana and Vincent had something to do with this, so pull the ribbon off the door and we'll find out together."

With little effort, she pulled the ribbon and it unfurled and fell on the floor. I turned my key in the lock with one hand and opened the door for her. She clicked on the lights and I followed her into our apartment. As soon as she stepped in the doorway, Vincent and his family yelled, "Surprise!" I stayed a little behind her and caught her as she was startled by the surprise and was swayed off her feet by the noise. I had the forethought to ask the doorman to bring up our bags, and he agreed to have them brought upstairs after noticing Lecia was a little unsteady on her feet. I kept my arms around her and nudged her into the door with my knees.

"Oh, my goodness. This *is* a surprise!" Her eyes widened, and she covered her mouth.

"Please don't tell me there are more baby gifts."

Dana and the children, Victor Alexander "Alex" age ten, Vivienne Alexis "Lexie" age seven and the twins Mitchell "Austin" and Marie Ariadne "Aria" three years old were gathered around and jumping up and down.

"No, we didn't bring more baby toys. We wanted to show you the renovations. Daddy even let us help tear down a few walls months ago." Alex added.

"We got to wear hard hats and heavy boots and you didn't know we were next door." Lexie came forward and hugged us while Aria and Austin urged us to come see all the changes. Our original apartment looked the same at the entrance, but the kitchen was expanded and filled with shiny new, gray steel appliances. We walked to the back of our home, formerly our neighbors' old apartment, and a dark stained heavy wood door stood where there was once a wall.

"Cade, why don't you open this door first?" Vincent suggested as his family looked on, but I wanted this to be special for Lecia to mark her first day back home.

"Lecia, why don't you do me the privilege of opening the door with me?" She clapped her hands, smiled at me, and opened the door. She stepped in, but my feet were frozen in place. I willed my body, but I couldn't move anything but my head as I canvassed the room.

"Is this why you kept the door locked Vincent?"

"Exactly. I wanted to keep prying eyes out of this room until it was completed, but I needed an acoustics engineer to work with me to design soundproof walls for your in-home studio, and he talked to one of the sound engineers at your studio who told us that this mixing console was like the one you used but a newer model. Do you plan to stand in the threshold all night bro, or come in and look around?"

Lecia grabbed my hand after I ran it through my hair and pulled on my roots as a check to see if I was awake. I felt the pain, so I wasn't caught up in a fantasy. I went and stood in front of the board, with its sleek microphones, a powerful computer with the latest recording software, and a keyboard for synthesizing and special effects. Looking to the side, I saw Vincent had designed an isolation booth behind a placement of drums and electric guitars and my award-winning albums were mounted on the wall. On the large desk I would use for my compositions was my favorite picture of Lecia.

"Do you like it?" Vincent stepped out of my view and I walked around the room I once dreamed of having as a young, budding musician. I had spoken to him years ago of owning my own home studio, where I could get lost in it for hours at a time if I wanted to, but I didn't want it at the cost of missing time with Lecia and the baby.

"You deserve this Cade. I'm so glad you finally got your home studio." Lecia answered my prayers with her blessings and kissed me on the lips.

"Say something, bro. Don't just stand there." I turned and did the only thing I could think of. I grabbed him by the shoulders in the tightest bear hug he could stand.

"If breaking a rib means you like it, I get it. You're ecstatic."

"Thank you, Vincent, Dana, and kids. The only thing that will make me happier is to hold my child in my arms for the first time." I took Lecia into my arms and kissed her good, but I held on to her to make sure she didn't trip before I touched her belly. Our son kicked back at my hand.

"I think he likes it too."

The kids were growing impatient and began coaxing Lecia to walk through the other rooms. There was another blue ribbon tied to the room across the hall from our new bedroom.

"Open the door, Tia Lecia." Aria jumped up and down, unable to stand the excitement any longer. She helped Lecia pull the ribbon off the door, and they stepped inside the brightly colored room with blue walls and a cream-colored crib with a blue cotton canopy mounted above it. There was space in the corner of the room for a reading nook in the near future, and wooden cabinets mounted on the walls around the room were filled with the menagerie of every stuffed animal imaginable looking down on us. Near the window, covered in coordinating fabric to match the crib, was an oversized rocking chair with comfortable padded material to bide away the time. Her desk contained supplies for nursing the baby, and a small refrigerator was in the corner.

"There's something else for you to see Tia Lecia, right Mommy?" Austin took Lecia by the hand and led her in front of another closed door. She opened it, and it was her private office with her medical equipment, her voluminous medical books, a media center to teleconference with her colleagues or attend telemedical trainings, and a computer set upon her desk. The walls were filled with her degrees and numerous clinical awards.

"Cade told me you planned to return to your practice at least part time after you had some time to bond with the baby, and he thought you might need space to maintain your professional development." Vincent showed her the desk and turned on the computer for her.

"I've always kept a home office to keep up with the ever-changing field of journalism. I love being a mother, but you don't have to give up everything to be a good mother." Dana piped in her support to encourage Lecia to remain engaged in her profession.

This time Lecia was speechless as she looked around at how much our living space had been transformed. I was no longer afraid of change and the new adventures the future would hold for us.

Michele Sims

CHAPTER EIGHT

"Lecia! Lecia, are you home?" I called out to her as I opened the door and stepped into our apartment with Vincent, who had picked me up from the airport and stayed at the club for the jam session. I dropped my bags at the door, jubilant to return home from a few appearances to begin promoting the album, and tonight I had an unexpected bonus of being on stage with musical legends.

"That's odd. It's not like Lecia to go to bed and leave all the lights on."

Considering it was late, and with the baby coming soon, I had become accustomed to her going to bed early, so I brushed away my initial concerns.

"Let me take your coat and you can move the baby items on floor to make a place for your satchel while I go check on Lecia and let her know we're here."

"Why are you trying to wake her up? Let her sleep while we unwind from a long night. What can I fix you to drink? I'll keep it light. Man, you were on fire tonight. Your last set was fantastic." Vincent patted me on the back.

He went to the bar to fix himself a cocktail, and even though I was still a little uneasy about the condition of the apartment, I decided to join him in a celebratory drink. The album was due to drop soon, and the cuts we performed tonight had been well received by the sold-out crowd.

"Make me a vodka on the rocks." I kicked back on the couch, relieved the promotional events was over.

Vincent's phone was buzzing nonstop.

"Someone is trying to get you. Is there something going on?"

He grabbed his phone and listened to the voicemail messages blowing up his phone.

"It's you brother. You're blowing up the news wire. The early reviews are in. Cade Moore, the man's on fire. An electrifying performance by Fortune tonight. If you weren't there, you missed a treat. Someone taped bits of the concert, and folks are commenting enthusiastically on your performance. One of the critics made an early declaration that your album was sure to be jazz album of the year. You won't be disappointed purchasing the album *Live at the Jazz Center-Cade Moore and Fortune*, he reported. The people have spoken brother, and I think you were a hit. I agree your performance tonight was memorable. You were in rare air tonight, Cade."

The members of Fortune weren't expecting to play tonight, but the headliner for the gala charitable event tonight got caught in a weather delay, and we went on as a favor to him. I thought we would be warming up the crowd, but never in my wildest dreams did I think we would do the entire show until after we were told his plane had been delayed and he'd missed his connection. This was an enormous break for the band. We had a good following of fans and had received critical acclaim from previous albums, but tonight allowed us the national exposure we were looking for. Movers and shakers in the music industry were there, and tonight was our breakout performance. I couldn't be a happier man. My band was riding a professional high and I was floating on a bright, fluffy, beautiful white cloud with all my good fortune.

I had a kind, loving, sexy wife, and my son was on his way. Lecia was due to give birth next week. Her doctor said it could be any day now, and there were days when the anticipation of a new member of the family coming into the world excited me beyond measure. I threw back the remainder of my drink, happy with my success, but I still had a gnawing feeling something wasn't right. My home felt different, and there was a metallic smell in the air like the smell of blood pooling on my face when I wasn't being careful with a sharp razor. Vincent was still savoring his drink with his feet up on the table when he looked down at the floor and saw small drops of blood.

"What's that on the floor? Did you have another accident with the electric saw? I told you I would help you with the installation of additional equipment in your studio."

"I didn't have an accident." I placed my glass on the table and got up.

"I need to check on Lecia, I'll be right back. I know she's literally heavy with child and may have just fallen asleep, but something doesn't feel right." My heart was beating fast and my hands trembled in my pockets as I surveyed the room.

"I'll be right back."

I traveled the length of the hall and opened the door to our bedroom. The lights and the television were on, and I saw Lecia covered up in bed, but she was very still and turned on her side.

"Lecia! Babe are you alright?"

I ran to her, my heart pounding in my ears, and sweat broke out across my brow. My chest was heaving, and my nose flared as the metallic smell of blood became more evident as I got closer to her. I stepped on sticky gauze material scattered across the floor, mottled and bright red with blood and there was a mound of towels covered in blood near the bed. Racing to her side as fast as I could, I heard a voice screaming into the air that sounded like a very scared version of me, calling out her name, willing her to move.

"Lecia, Lecia!" Her eyes were closed and her arms, splattered with thick blood, slipped out of my hand and fell back to the pillow, as if she were a lifeless rag doll.

"Oh God, oh God. Please don't let her die."

Vincent came running into the room and froze by her bedside. It was as if time just stopped around us as we surveyed the room in a whirlwind haze of images foreign to the bedroom I shared with my wife: a shiny gray pole with an IV bag still hanging from it, blood-soaked gloves thrown on the side of the bed opposite Lecia, a capped needle with a small amount of liquid still in the syringe, and blood-soaked silver surgical scissors and scalpels on a small, soiled silver tray on the nightstand. I pulled the stained covers off my wife who was motionless on the bed and unresponsive to my touch. Time sped up again as Vincent was on the opposite side of the bed checking for a pulse high on her neck. He opened her lids and her pupils weren't blown.

"Cade, she has a pulse. We have to get her help quickly."

She was very pale, but her chest rose slowly as she continued to take shallow breaths. I gently rolled her on her back and saw what I dreaded in addition to this gruesome scene. The beautiful mound on her abdomen where my son had rested in her uterus was no longer there. Lecia had a hospital gown thrown loosely across her shoulders, and it draped over the concavity of her barren womb. I pulled the gown off her shoulders and, in disbelief, I saw her naked body, with loose, flaccid skin over her belly.

"Cade, help is on the way." I looked at Vincent with his phone plastered to his ear. He was sweating profusely while attempting to reassure me and listen to the person on the line. He checked for a pulse again.

"Slow and weak. Yeah, she's breathing on her own. Alright, I'll do it." He placed the phone on the bed.

"Cade, I need to pull back the gown, so I can give a report of what's going on here. OK? Do you understand? We need to do an exam of her pelvis."

I shook my head and gave my brother implicit permission to pull back the gown covering my wife's naked body, and I helped him gently pull Lecia's legs apart. It was like an out-of-body experience, and I was somewhere hovering high at the ceiling giving my physical body strength to avoid vomiting or passing out.

We looked between her legs saw her vagina covered with gauze. I pushed that to the side, revealing that someone had recently placed stitches there. She was not actively bleeding, and Vincent pressed with light pressure on her abdomen to assess the area where my boy had once grown inside her just hours before this nightmare. He covered her back with the gown and picked up his phone.

"The baby is gone. Yes, I'll search the apartment to make sure he's not here." He hung up the phone and rubbed his hand through his hair, now clumped together with Lecia's blood.

"Lecia, hold on. Cade, they said they're worried she is going into shock and of course there's the concern about infection. I'm going to check the apartment and you stay here with her." I nodded, grabbed her hand, and began stroking her hair.

"Stay with me sweetheart. Please don't leave me."

There were bruises on her face and shoulders. Her lips were bleeding and swollen, all signs of a struggle before she was subdued, and there was blood and tissue under her nails.

I stroked the side of her face and began coming out of my state of shock as I witnessed evidence my sweet Lecia had been beaten and abused. My cold emotions were replaced by hot rage. Lecia tried to pull away, as the heat of my hand was causing her hand to redden and become wet with sweat.

"Lecia?" Her eyes fluttered for the first time.

"I promise you I'll find out who did this to us. I'll find our son and bring him back to us."

She didn't respond. My heart was beating fast and I started to experience a slight tremor in my hands. I shook my head, attempting to keep the thought at bay that I might have already lost my son and may be on the verge of losing my wife. Vincent came back to the bedside with an emergency response team behind him. I knew I was in the way, but I couldn't bear letting go of her hand. I couldn't bear the thought that she couldn't feel my love and support.

"We're going to need to start some lines before we transport her. Can you all step into the hall please?" the lead EMT communicated to us.

I heard Dana's voice and the sound of her footsteps approaching the room and he rushed to the door to block her view.

"Vincent Adam Moore, you left me a cryptic message and I get here and there's an ambulance waiting downstairs. Can you explain what's going on? You promised me you would never take another assignment after Alex was born. How dare you go back on your word? I know what your phone message to me means. Dana, I don't know when I'll be home means you're on another assignment."

She stopped speaking and tilted her head to look inside the bedroom as we silently observed the synchronized actions of the emergency personnel starting IV lines and connecting Lecia to monitors. Dana was wide eyed, afraid, and her traumatized brain had her mute at first before she fully registered that something horrible had happened to Lecia in our bedroom, who was motionless except for the actions of medical personnel moving her body to prepare her for transport.

"What happened to Lecia? Where's the baby? When did you find her? Why didn't you tell me what was going on? Have you called the police?" Vincent took his wife outside of the bedroom and urged me to followed them out to the hall, but I stayed within sight of the action in the bedroom. Dana started crying and shaking in Vincent's arms as he attempted to console her.

I was torn between going with Lecia and staying behind to find the predators who had hurt her. I felt a murderous rage welling up inside my chest as Lecia was lifted off the bed and placed on the stretcher.

"We need to get her to the nearest emergency room. She's going into shock," the lead EMT told us and we answered as many of their questions as we could. I told them she was eight and a half months pregnant but that someone had delivered the baby and abducted him. Vincent turned to Dana and tried to answer her questions.

"Dana, I'm not accepting an assignment, but I need my friends to help me. Please go in the ambulance with Lecia while I talk to Cade before he meets her at the hospital. It's critical we gather as much evidence as possible as soon as possible. The baby's life may depend on our quick action."

She agreed and left with Lecia in the ambulance. Although I knew my brother was involved in a shadowy syndicate of government officials, captains of industry, and assassins known as the Network, I didn't know that Dana was aware of his involvement in the organization.

"She knows?" I asked after Dana departed with Lecia.

"She knows a little about my involvement, and I want to keep it that way. I didn't tell you that I set up a security system in your apartment while you and Lecia were on your honeymoon. I guess the excitement of the holidays and the good news that Lecia was pregnant contributed to my memory lapse."

"You bugged my apartment? Really, Vincent? Man, have you heard of the concepts of privacy and boundaries?"

"Cade, you'll be glad I did it. Don't worry. I'm not a voyeur; there are no cameras in your bedroom. I never looked at the feed on the system, and I'll only go back to the last few hours to see who may have been in the apartment with Lecia. In the meantime, can you get some things together for her and the baby to take to the hospital. I need your behavior to be above suspicion. You'll need to stay at the hospital with Lecia while I take care of this matter." I stepped back, startled at his suggestion.

I shouldn't avenge my wife and you need to do it? "You must have lost your mind if you think I'm not going to search for my son."

I stormed off to grab Lecia's bag while Vincent went to examine the footage on the security system. I hadn't noticed it before, but there was a typed letter on the dresser, and I returned to the front of the apartment with it.

"Vincent, I discovered this typed letter warning me not to call the police."

"Let me see it." He took it out of my hand and read it quickly before going to the side of the room and removing the large picture of a beach scene on the wall to reveal a metal safe containing the security system. He pressed in his code on the steel door, activating the *view footage* component of the system, and picked up his satchel on the couch.

"I'm downloading the information to my tablet. While I'm doing that, place the letter in a safe place. It will be the cover we need to explain why we didn't contact the police." He opened his leather satchel and took out his computer tablet while I placed the letter in a drawer. His affiliation with the Network allowed him access to the most advanced technological equipment before it reached the mass market.

I joined him on the couch and hoped the recorded images provided us with answers of what had happened here. He opened the download, and the high-resolution images of a pregnant Lecia walking around the apartment came on the screen. She turned her attention to the door, walked across the room, and looked through the peephole. A look of surprise spread across her face and she opened the door to a smiling Mario, Marco's older brother. She hugged him and invited him inside.

Vincent fast-forwarded the images of scenes that turned from friendly to sinister as the recorded frames flowed by from zero to twenty minutes into the visit. Mario seemed more uncomfortable after he pulled out a white wadded cotton cloth from his pocket and hid it from Lecia's view. She returned from the kitchen with a glass of water for him and turned her back, allowing him to take her by surprise and grab her around the shoulders. She was yelling something; I couldn't make out what she was saying without an audio feed. She scratched his face and he slapped her causing her head to recoil backwards before he placed the white cloth to her mouth and nose. I slammed my fists down on the table while Vincent held fast to the tablet.

"Cade, I know this is difficult, but we've got to finish watching this for evidence in recovering the baby."

"I swear I'm going to fillet his ass when I catch him."

"Calm down please bro'." He looked at me and I took deep breaths before we resumed watching the recording, where I saw Lecia struggling against him until she succumbed from the substance he held against her nose and mouth. Her eyes rolled in the back of her head and then she slid down his leg, unconscious.

He picked her up, her arms flailing while he struggled in his attempt to bear her weight and carry her to the bedroom. He came back out of the bedroom to the front area of the apartment seconds later in full view of the camera and picked up the phone to call someone.

"That bastard. I'm going to peel his flesh from his bones and burn it."

"Calm down Cade; we need to keep our heads if we're going to teach him a lesson."

Vincent fast-forwarded the feed again and saw Mario go to the door and open it for Darlene Evans. She had a suitcase in her hand and looked in the direction of the camera. She appeared to say, "Where is the bitch with my baby?" Mario pointed to my bedroom as he pulled hospital equipment inside. My jaw slackened; I couldn't believe what was unfolding before my eyes.

"Vincent, I don't believe this shit! Darlene is a nurse practitioner and I'm sure she swore an oath to do no harm. Lecia was once her best friend, and she's helping this piece of shit? What did he have on her?" Vincent pressed pause to answer my question.

"I don't know Cade. This is unbelievable, but we need to focus. I don't want to miss any clues that may lead us to the recovery of the baby. Don't worry—the two of them are going to pay." I knew my brother had a darkness in him no sane person would ever want to encounter. His face was red, and his jaw pulsed, tight and determined. I felt the hostility in his statement, and it made me return my attention to the tape. Vincent had already resumed looking at the footage after taking the tape off pause.

We watched as Darlene set up an IV and pulled up some medication in a syringe with a needle attached. Several recorded hours went by, and we fast-forwarded the tape until we saw Darlene emerge with my son wrapped in his blue blanket. She left with the baby while Mario placed some of the evidence of their crime in a closet in the far corner of the front room. I was so angry that the veins on the back of my hands were visible and looked like hardened ropes of vessels filled with the hot blood coursing through my body. My face was so warm from the blood rushing to my head that I thought I would combust if my pressure went up any further and my vision was blurred. I clenched my fists and started to pace the room, trying to gather my thoughts and decide on my course of action. I was on my way to get my gun when Vincent got in my face and ordered that I stick with the plan to go to the hospital with Lecia.

"Vincent, I don't want to argue with you, but I never said I agreed with your plan. I may have plans of my own, big brother."

"Kaiden, I know you're angry, but I need your cooperation. We don't have time to waste."

"Lecia is my wife; and my son is missing, so I get to decide how I want to handle this." Vincent got in my face again to stop my advance toward the case where I stored my gun. He refused to move aside, and I attempted to shove him, but he placed me in a choke hold.

"I don't want to do this, but I won't release you if you refuse to listen."

He loosened his hold on me and placed his hands on my shoulder before I pulled away. I was aware of my brother's moves from years of wrestling with him. I knew he was going to try to take me down and pin me, but I escaped his grasp. He lunged toward me and we both went down on the floor. He attempted to gain control, but I countered all his moves and I was busy defending myself, so I didn't realize the front door had opened and he finally overpowered me with assistance from two burly guys. It took all of them to take me down since, with my rage intensified by adrenaline, I still had the strength to make it difficult.

"Cade don't make this more difficult than it has to be."

I was held upside down in the arms of one of Vincent's goons with my legs pinned. He dropped me on the floor, and I slipped away and managed to get to my feet when I heard my mother yelling at all of us. We must have looked like a mangled mess of bodies sweating and struggling with each other for control.

"Charles Aiden make them stop. I can't believe they would pick a difficult time like this to fight each other."

I stopped struggling to get away after my mother began yelling at us. I had barely caught my breath after Goon Number One let me down. Vincent came closer and helped me up as I managed to share my frustrations with my parents. I was talking through my teeth trying to hold back tears.

"It's my family who has been hurt. Why are you always so comfortable with Vincent being the family's hero?" I felt Vincent release the tight grip he had on me as I gathered my wits about me and pushed him away.

"Brother, you're the one who has the most difficult assignment. I'll go search for those bastards and find your son, but you'll be the one who has to tell Lecia the baby is gone."

The weight of his statement fell on me. I was stunned as I realized Lecia probably didn't know what happened to her. *Gone, as in dead?*

I dropped my head, which felt too heavy to bear on my neck. I felt spineless, and my shoulders slumped as I felt I had nothing in me I could use to help Lecia.

"Gone for now Cade. I need your help, so I can change our current reality. We've always been there for each other, and we've never let each other down, but I need you to do your part. You need to tell Lecia when she wakes up what happened."

I was the one who would have to look into her eyes and try to hide the possibility that we may never see our son alive again. I refused to think about that possibility, but the grief of it overwhelmed me. I knew I had finally given in to the enormity of the horrific tragedy, but I didn't remember when my tears started to fall as if a tsunami of grief had hit me or when my parents encircled me in an embrace to comfort me. Everything was so hazy, but I heard Vincent remind me to go to the hospital and let him handle the rest. He gave me a bag with a burner cellphone and told me he would contact me with frequent updates. We didn't talk about the involvement of the Network in front of our parents, but I knew the Network could manage a thorough investigation of this crime. I drew strength from knowing that if anyone could find my son, the agents in the Network had the highest likelihood of finding him alive. The shadowy organization had been involved in many covert operations around the world, including the return of high-profile individuals who had been kidnapped. I knew Vincent would have already activated the cell of the undercover agents needed to assist us with this operation.

"I promise I'll cooperate Vincent." I looked at my parents. "How did you know what happened?" My father took his hand off my shoulder and answered.

"We were in town and caught a little of your performance. Dana called to tell us that something horrible happened to Lecia, but she didn't share much of the details with your mother. She suggested we come to the apartment before heading to the hospital. I'm glad she told us. Things may have really gotten out of control here and I know you don't want to hear this but, we agree with your brother. We don't want you to commit a crime or be a suspect in a crime. I think you can understand that right now you need to be with Lecia. Are you ready to go? Do you have some things for her?"

"Yes, I plan to take the bag she packed for her and the baby. I'm ready to go." I stiffened my shoulders to gather my pride and smoothed out the wrinkles and fist marks on my clothes that remained following my encounter with my brother and his security team.

"Tell Dana, I'll call her as soon as I can. She knows the routine. When I'm concerned about safety issues, she knows a security team gets assigned to her and the kids. Please expect that some men will be outside of Lecia's suite when she's transferred from intensive care."

He placed his hands on my shoulders and looked me in the eyes.

"Cade you've always been there for me and my family. Let me do this for you and your family. I love Lecia and my nephew and I take this evil act personally. Brother, trust me, we both will have justice." He patted me on the shoulder and whispered in my ear, "And revenge."

"Call me, Vincent…I'm sorry for what I said about you claiming the spotlight. The truth is, you are the family hero." He gave me a quick hug.

"We're brothers and that's the only thing that matters right now after making sure Lecia and the baby are alright."

He waved goodbye as I grabbed the bag and went to the door, followed by my parents. I was considering how I was going to tell Lecia what had happened to us. I looked back and Vincent had already taken a seat to view the tape with his security team. I still thought they looked like goons.

We walked down the hall and waited for the elevator doors to open while my mother patted my arm.

"Cade, you do know it's best that Vincent wait for the police to come to answer questions for their investigation. We're all here to help, and that doesn't make Vincent the family hero."

"Yeah, Mom. I was just spouting off in anger." *What is taking the elevator so long to get here?*

"It's curious none of the officers have arrived yet. Dana told us it was a gruesome scene in the bedroom. You're sure Vincent alerted the authorities? I know you were more concerned about getting Lecia to the hospital." My father looked on but remained silent. I leaned forward and pressed the button to call the elevator, impatient to get on our way.

"The authorities were notified." *I wasn't lying.*

Vincent had called the team he knew would help find my child by any means necessary. We didn't have time for rules, policies, and procedures and I couldn't tolerate an interrogation of too many questions and not enough answers—not now. The elevator finally came, the doors opened, and I escorted my parents into the elevator. This was as gritty as my life had ever been. The sound of the elevator seemed loud and tortuous as we made our way to the ground floor. Something as mundane as going down in an elevator in New York now felt like I had entered a torture chamber on my way to the house of horrors. Here I was, almost twenty-seven, and I hadn't liked hospitals since my parents took me to the emergency room at four years old after I'd broken my collarbone. I grabbed my shoulder, suddenly throbbing with a phantom pain.

Sweat popped out on my brow as the dark pall of a foreboding death descended upon me and made my skin feel hot, then cool and clammy. I brushed all thoughts of death out of my mind because I was choosing life. I couldn't lose Lecia or my son. My life and my sanity depended on it and we needed to get to the hospital as soon as possible.

CHAPTER NINE

My father's limo driver knew where to take us. Racing to the nearest hospital, he got there in no time and turned at the red neon sign emblazoned with a cross and the words boldly written in block letters: Emergency Entrance. He came to a quick stop in the driveway and we got out to head for the glass sliding doors.

Flashing red lights from multiple ambulances coming up from behind encircled us and bounced off the glass walls, lighting up the darkness. We were pushed to the side by grim-faced emergency-room personnel running to greet patients with bloodied faces staring wide eyed and frightened on stretchers. We moved over and allowed them the right of way while the loud sound of emergency sirens pierced our ears, causing a reverberation lasting minutes at a time. I covered my ears as the attendant standing at the double doors pointed to the non-emergency entrance for visitors. The irony of the situation wasn't lost on me as my parents smartly dressed in tailored black evening attire joined me in entering the trauma center entrance, where we were assaulted by the sights and smells of all sorts of fluids emanating from injured human bodies in the waiting area. My mother placed her hand above her lips to cover her nose as we made our way to the check-in desk.

"More incoming, bad traffic accident with multi-car collisions," I overheard one staff member yell to another other before they ran to meet the next ambulance rolling in. Staff members called over the loudspeaker raced to help in the emergency room to assist. I looked at the custodians placing signs to avoid wet areas as they mopped the floors and splashed antiseptic cleaning solution on the floors, filling the space with strong smells. The sights and smells were overstimulating, but I steadied myself and stopped to locate the check-in desk in this fast-paced setting. People filled the chairs and every available space against the walls.

I made it to the counter and the young woman who sat stone-faced at the desk had no time for smiles or conventional niceties.

"Can I help you?"

"I'm Cade Moore, and I'm looking for my wife, Alicia Moore. She was brought here by ambulance."

She looked up Lecia's name and found her on the computer. "She's been admitted and moved to the ICU."

I returned to my parents waiting a short distance behind me, and we got directions to Elevator A, the most direct route to the ICU.

"Mom, please don't mention anything about the baby to Lecia." She placed her hand over her mouth and, for the first time since this saga began, Mom dropped a few tears.

"What if the police have already come to question her? You should say something." The elevator doors opened, and we entered the space with calm mood music piped in.

"I don't think they have had a chance to come to the hospital."

"You seem so sure of it, Cade. Did Vincent tell you he would call after they spoke to him and since they haven't, you think they haven't talked to her?"

"It's just a feeling I have, but if I'm wrong, let me feel her out. I want to keep her as calm as possible." The doors opened, and we began our walk down another long corridor with an antiseptic smell, but it was less assaultive to my senses. Another set of double doors with signs on it stood between us and the ICU, with specific instructions on the visiting hours and the number of visitors allowed.

Dana came outside the intensive care unit wearing a sticker with her visitor credentials just as we arrived. Her eyes were red and swollen from crying, and she came and hugged me and my father, then went to my mother and cried in her arms for a few moments.

"She hasn't opened her eyes and she's not very responsive. The doctors are waiting to talk to you. You came at the right time."

"Thank you, Dana, for being there for us. We're here now. Why don't you go home and get some rest and I promise I'll call if there are changes in Lecia's condition. The kids will be worried if both you and Vincent are gone."

"I'm glad I could be there for you. You're right. I need to be strong, and I don't want to upset the children. Please don't forget to call me. I'll go gather my things."

"I promise," I assured her as she went to the waiting room attendant to get her things and we prepared to go see Lecia.

I pressed the intercom button to announce our arrival, and the security door opened, allowing us entrance into the ICU. The doctor awaited our arrival, and there were nurses monitoring Lecia, who was hooked up to machines around her bed. We took turns kissing her on the cheek and then turned to the doctor, who shook our hands as we introduced ourselves.

"Let me start with the good news. She is breathing on her own and hasn't required a ventilator since she's been here. Her vital signs have stabilized with fluids she received, and she has also gotten a pint of blood. We'll continue to monitor her and consider an EEG in the next twenty-four hours if she remains unresponsive. The results of her blood tests, which included a toxicology screen from a national CSI lab, were sent to us here at the hospital, and I wasn't sure how we got the results so fast, but it showed she had a mixture of drugs in her system." I nodded and knew Vincent and his team had something to do with getting results from the exclusive lab.

"It appears that Mrs. Moore was given a toxic cocktail to induce labor, a hallucinogen, and a sedative, which we consider the main reason for us to expect she'll remain sedated for the next twenty-four hours. She may also begin hallucinating." He took in a deep breath before he continued.

"The examination of her uterus showed that the baby was delivered and her placenta, the afterbirth, was no longer in place. She was brutally assaulted and may have no recollection of what happened to her. Mr. Moore, do you want the nurses to administer a medication that will begin the process of drying up her breast milk? It will be painful for her with engorged breasts without a baby to nurse as I understand he was abducted and his whereabouts unknown."

"No, that won't be necessary." I grabbed the railing of Lecia's bed and stroked her hair, adamant I didn't want that to happen. Lecia looked forward to feeding our baby, and I couldn't lose hope that she would be given the opportunity to breastfeed our child. I held her hand to reassure her.

"When her breast milk comes in, we'll manually express it and hopefully soon she can make her own decision regarding the matter. A sample of the milk we obtained has been given to the lab for analysis, and only a faint amount of the drugs were found in her breast milk. I feel comfortable we'll be able to flush out the toxins remaining in her breast milk if her kidneys continue to function well. Do you have any questions for me?"

"No, I think you've given us a thorough explanation of Lecia's condition for now." We shook hands again and the doctor left. I leaned over the railing, kissed Lecia again, and held her hand firmly in mine. I looked at my mother, who was being comforted by my father.

"Lecia's parents will start to worry if they don't hear from her. She calls them every morning. Could you call Marisela to tell her that Lecia is being observed for premature labor?"

"Cade, I don't think I should lie to Lecia's parents. I wouldn't want them to lie to us." She looked up at my father for support and he nodded in agreement.

"Mom, Papi is still very weak. He can't travel just yet. It would kill him to know what happened to Lecia and the baby. Just buy me some time while I figure something out."

"I understand Cade." My mother hesitated but eventually agreed. She searched through her pocketbook to find her personal phone book.

"I'll call them now. Charles Aiden, will you come with me?" They got up to go to a private area to make the phone call.

They were gone for several minutes and I looked up and saw Vincent through the glass window walking toward the room. He stopped to reach into his bag to take a phone call, then came in, hugged me briefly, and went to the bedside to look at Lecia.

"Where's Dana, Mom, and Dad?"

"I sent Dana home to be with the kids after we arrived. I didn't want them to wake up and discover both parents were gone and only the nanny there who couldn't explain what was happening. Mom and Dad are calling Lecia's parents to tell them the partial truth. Mom agreed to help me buy some time before I tell them the whole story. I don't think Papi would survive if he knew the truth."

"Good deal Cade. Let me fill you in before Mom and Dad return. I had the team go over your apartment in minute detail, and the tape was also reviewed several times. We saw that Mario was smoking and left a matchbook with the name of a downtown hotel on it. We called and found out he was indeed checked in to that hotel. The owners of your building allowed us to look at the security footage in front of the building and it showed the cab that Darlene used to depart. The driver recalled the woman who left early in the morning with an infant, and he took her to the same hotel. We apprehended Darlene and she thinks she was picked up by the police, but it was Network operatives who discovered her and are posing as the police."

I was on the edge of my seat. It was evident to me that there was a significant omission; he hadn't told me that they found my son or Mario.

"We haven't located the baby or Mario yet, but Darlene is still delusional that there's a chance the two of you will get back together to raise the baby. That woman is sick."

Vincent continued to talk while my parents were still out of the room on the phone with Lecia's parents. I turned to Lecia, who had her eyes closed, but I felt her attempting to grab my hand.

"Don't worry Lecia. We're going to get our baby back." I squeezed her hand again.

"Cade, I need you to muster as much strength as you can to participate in a ruse I've concocted. We gave her a cellphone with the hope that her one phone call will be to you—she asked for your number—so you'll need to keep the phone I gave you on. She thinks one of the security guards agreed to slip her the contraband phone for a price after she offered him money and if desired, sex. I need you to tell her you were considering leaving Lecia to be with her and you must convince her she has a chance with you. Can you do that?"

"What the shit are you saying? I hate that bitch. You really want me to tell her I want to be with her and mean it?"

"Yes, that's exactly what I'm saying. I want you to be as believable as possible, even if it means going to her in person and kissing her."

My cellphone started ringing and I opened my bag and looked at the number, which was unfamiliar to me. The call went to voicemail and I opened the message. There was an attachment with a picture of a newborn baby with greenish-brown eyes. The phone was shaking in my hands and Vincent took it from me and read the message out loud.

"I'm in New York and Mario had a picture of a newborn delivered to me earlier. He told me to think about the possibility of getting back together with my ex-wife and raising this boy as my own. He said he knew the mother and she didn't want the child. He thought that if I had a son and told my ex I had adopted him, she would return to me and Mami would be happy to have a grandchild. I'm almost too frightened to ask. Is this Lecia's baby? My brother hates you, but I can't imagine he hates you enough to hurt Lecia."

Vincent explained why Marco may have contacted me. "We located Marco and initially thought he was an accomplice but decided against that possibility, as he looked so shit-faced when we told him what Mario had done and he agreed to help. I gave him equipment to contact me if he heard from Mario again." Vincent texted him.

Vincent: Yes, that's Lecia's son.

"I'm going to assume this is your baby. We can't be sure until he's tested, but he looks so much like Austin as a newborn, only with greenish-brown eyes instead of brown eyes." The phone buzzed again with another message from Marco.

> **Marco**: Mario told me to meet him later today. He'll let me know the time and place that I can find the baby.

> **Vincent:** Good.

"Marco has said repeatedly he had nothing to do with this heinous plan and he'll stay in contact. We'll find out soon if he's lying. I had a tail placed on him." Vincent continued.

"I can't say I trust him." My phone went off again and this time it was Darlene. I took a deep breath before answering it.

"Hello? Is this you my darlin'?" Darlene's voice was syrupy and slurred, and she was talking as if we were old friends and maybe past lovers.

"This is Cade."

"Oh Cade. I'm so glad you answered my call. Baby, I need you. I'm in trouble, but I promise I did everything so that we could be together. I need to tell you some good news. We have a son. I can't talk too long, but I couldn't wait to hear your voice."

I grabbed my abdomen to stop from hurling the bile that was roiling inside me.

This bitch is delusional. Vincent motioned for me to settle down. I took in a breath and sat back in my chair to prepare for the performance of my life.

"She's been given sedatives. One good turn deserves another." Vincent whispered to me and I turned my attention back to Darlene.

"We have a beautiful son, Cade. I need you to come, get me and then we can recover our boy." I listened in silence. "Cade are you there?"

"Yes, I'm still here. What makes you think we can be together with our son? What son are you talking about?" I said through gritted teeth.

"Cade believe me. He is the most beautiful child with the deepest hazel eyes. He looks so much like you, and he's your son."

"You're telling me you were pregnant, and I have a son that looks like me somewhere out there?" *But I never had sex with you.*

"Yes, that's exactly what I'm telling you. You don't need Lecia to bear children for you. I'm here to give you what you want and need." I pulled the phone away from my ear and looked at it in disbelief.

"Your timing is perfect Darlene. I've been giving some thought to leaving Lecia. We weren't as compatible as I once thought. Things weren't working out between us because she doesn't understand me like you do."

"Cade, you don't know how happy I am to hear that."

"Maybe you can help me understand why Lecia's friend Marco contacted me—you remember him from our wedding, don't you?"

"Yes, I vaguely remember him from that sham of a wedding you had with Lecia."

"Well he sent a picture of a baby boy to me who he claims is his son. He wanted to let us know how happy he was after the birth of his son this morning. Let me forward the picture to you. I must admit, the baby is cute."

I was in such emotional pain, but I had to continue the conversation. I heard someone in the background telling Darlene that she didn't have much more time on the phone. I forwarded the picture to her and heard her gasp on the other end. She must have received the picture.

"That bastard Mario. He stole my baby—our baby. That double-crossing bastard. Where are you right now?"

I thought about my response. "I slept at the club. I was exhausted after the performance last night."

"So you haven't gone home yet?"

"No Darlene. Lecia and I had an argument before I left for the promotional tour. You know Lecia has a pattern of walking out on me when she's angry."

"Good. I need money for bail and I don't have enough in my account. I promise I'll make it worth your while if you help me. If you deposit money in my account, I'll tell you where to find our son, but I'm not sure what floor of the hotel he's on. His babysitter has him and she'll release him when I call. We can meet at the airport and leave New York forever." I was holding my breath and Vincent struck me on the arm and reminded me to keep going.

"Darlene you need to cover your tracks and resign from your position at the hospital. That way no one will contact the authorities to look for you. I can go to your apartment and gather some things for you, but I'll need to get your security code to get into your apartment. You don't have to tell me anything else until you're sure the funds were deposited into your account. I promise I'll have the funds wired to you, but I can't come in person to the station because I don't want Lecia to think that we're back together. We don't have a prenup and I'm sure she'll be very vindictive if she knew I left her for you. She won't grant me a divorce and we won't be able to be together."

I let her ponder her options and waited silently while she thought about my proposal and finally, she took the bait. Vincent pulled out his tablet and wired the money into her account.

"Hold on Cade, one of the guards needs to talk to me. I'll need to mute the phone but don't hang up."

"I won't." I looked over at Lecia to get strength to continue. Vincent continued looking over all the monitors to make sure the notification sounds were off. Darlene worked in a hospital and the sounds would have been familiar to her. She returned to the phone after a few minutes.

"Cade, I'm back. Are you still there? I can't believe you sent me this much money? I have never seen an account this large with my name on it. Someone from the bank called my cellphone to let me know a large amount of money had been deposited into my account. Wait, something funny is going on here. The police said the branch manager called me on my personal cell phone and he wasn't all that interested in me when I went into the bank earlier this month to get a loan, and by the way, how did you get my account number?"

I laughed. "You were at the club so much and you purchased so many tickets to see my shows with your debit card that I asked my manager to get your account number and I dumped the money into your account as a security bond of love and faith between us. A friend of mine by chance witnessed your arrest and called me to tell me about it. I've pulled some strings to let my friends at the station know you're with me and to treat you well until we can get you out of this mess."

Vincent gave me two thumbs up as I started to hurl again. Leave it to my brother to think about all angles. I hoped I could stay one step ahead of Darlene, who was twisted but no dummy.

"Cade, darling, that was so sweet of you. I didn't ask but, are you ok?"

"Yes, I'm excited we'll be together finally."

"I'll call the babysitter who has been taking care of the baby before I run out of time and the guards return. They told me my boyfriend must have friends in high places, as it was unusual for them to leave a prisoner alone for long periods of time in an interrogation room, but I don't trust them. They are probably coming back now so I need you to listen to me. Go to the Bradley Hotel, and the baby is either in rooms twelve ninety-eight, twelve eighty-four or twelve forty-eight. I don't want them to follow me there after I'm released. Things are moving so fast and I can't remember exactly where that double-crossing M—I mean where I took the baby. I wanted the added protection of having someone available to take care of the baby while I returned to my apartment to get some things, so I hired a babysitter. Hurry darlin' and bring our son to me. I usually fly out of the international gate at LaGuardia, and I'll meet you at the airport as soon as I post bail. I'm not sure what they are charging me with, but with the large amount of money you sent, I shouldn't have any problem getting out. There are many flights leaving all day, so we can decide where we want to go, fly out separately, and then meet up somewhere in paradise. I can't wait to be with you and our son. Pick up the phone when I call again. Bye my dear."

"Bye, sweetheart. See you soon."

Vincent was keying the numbers into his computer as I wrote them down.

"The managers of the hotel have been very helpful, and the location of the room was already narrowed down to the eleventh to thirteenth floors. They can now focus on the twelfth floor as they continue to look at the hotel's security video. Mario was picked up on video getting on the elevator leaving his room and going to another room, but he was smart enough to wander around several floors with the baby before going to the second room. But I promise, we'll eventually get him too."

Vincent picked up his stuff and bolted out the room before I could ask him more questions. He met our parents returning to the room and was careful to grab our mother and kiss her before running out.

"Gotta go. Talk to you later." He waved goodbye and disappeared down the hall.

"Any news on the baby?" I didn't want to raise her hopes or give answers to questions that I couldn't answer.

"No, not yet." My father placed his arms around her shoulders.

"Lecia's parents were worried. They sensed that something was wrong, and they thought it curious that you didn't call them. They told us if there was renewed trouble in your relationship with Lecia, her friend Mario probably had something to do with it. They are very perceptive people and I felt so bad lying to them."

Lecia's nurse came in the room and I was happy for the distraction.

"We've been monitoring Mrs. Moore from the computer monitors at the nurses' station, and the doctors felt comfortable after the conference on her care plan to transfer her from her ICU room to a suite on the same floor in the stepdown unit. She's not as alert as we would like, but her vital signs are stable. She'll still be closely monitored, and her doctor will continue to follow her outside of the ICU." We thanked her for the good news and she departed.

An hour went by before the nurses from the stepdown unit received the report and came to transport Lecia to her new room. Her new treatment team must have had an affiliation with the Network because no one asked us about the baby, no one was disturbed that there were armed guards outside her room, and they seemed comfortable when they told us that an outside team of medical consultants had been called in to assist with her management.

"Cade, was it your idea or Vincent's to call in a specialist on Lecia's case? Your brother isn't a doctor, but I remember how many specialists he called in to assist with Mother's care," my mother asked from her seat at Lecia's bedside.

"We discussed it while he was here, and I agreed to it."

We entered the room in the new unit after they settled her in, and Lecia was still asleep in no apparent distress. The room, a suite located at the end of the corridor, was spacious, cheerful, and partitioned off. The other side contained amenities such as a sitting area, stuffed chairs, and a small kitchenette. I went to her bedside and kissed her, but she didn't respond to my voice or to my touch.

"Lecia, it's Cade. I love you sweetheart. I'm here for you and I won't leave you." Her eyelids fluttered, and she took a deep breath. My parents went to the other side of the bed and stroked her hand and her hair while telling her they loved her.

I looked at them both and they look exhausted. For the first time, I saw signs my parents were getting older. They were in great shape, but the stress of this situation was taking a toll on them.

"Why don't the two of you go back to your rental and get some rest. I would tell you to go to my place, but they're still treating it as a crime scene. I'll call if anything changes, I promise. I'll be ok, and I plan to stay with Lecia, camped out in the chairs over there. I'll try to take a nap before the next report from Lecia's team since we all need to take care of ourselves and stay strong for her."

My father placed his hands on my mother's shoulders.

"You're right Cade. Lauren has been up all night, and we both need to grab some sleep and come back to the hospital later today."

They hugged me before leaving, and I promised to call if I needed them. I pulled up a chair and sat close to Lecia. I kissed the back of her hand, and she started moving her head. I heard her say, "Ayudame Papi. Ayudame Mami." *Help me Papi. Help me Mami.* My heart broke for her and I wiped the tears from my eyes.

"Tengo miedo, Miguel. Ayudame, please." *I'm scared Miguel. Help me please.*

I grabbed her hands and got in the bed with her. She was calling for her deceased twin brother, and I needed to comfort her before I shattered into a thousand pieces. Vincent was right that this wasn't going to be easy. I took her in my arms and placed her head on my chest. Moments later she spoke again.

"I love you Cade. I love you more than life itself." She was talking but her eyes remained closed. A nurse came running in the room and didn't chastise me for being in her bed.

"Her blood pressure is rising." I sat up and was listening to the nurse when Lecia started to thrash about in the bed.

"I'm sorry Cade, I'm so sorry. Forgive me, please!" she started yelling and crying. I grabbed her and placed her in a tight embrace against my chest.

"I'll call her doctor and get an order for restraints. I don't think he wants to give her more meds."

"No, I won't consent to physical restraints."

She started to calm down, and I didn't let her go until she stopped fighting against me. I comforted her with words of love and with the steady beat of my heart I hoped she felt as she leaned against my chest.

"I love you and I don't blame you." She calmed down, opened her eyes, and spoke again, this time in whispers.

"Can't think, Cade." She paused before attempting to speak again. "Baby?"

I looked at her with tears welling up in my eyes. My mouth was dry, and my tongue was stuck to the roof of my mouth. I struggled for words as she looked into my eyes. My mind went blank as I searched for something comforting to say, and I saw her heavy lids come down. She was out again. Her head fell back slowly in my arms, and I cried as I kept her close in my arms. The nurse granted us privacy by backing out of the room and closing the door behind her. I slid down on the bed with Lecia in my arms and rested with her on my chest.

"Stay with me Lecia. I need you. I love you." She didn't respond to me anymore, and I knew she was tired and needed to rest.

Committing myself to telling her the truth with as much compassion as I could if she asked about the baby again, I calmed myself with the reassurance that I would find the words to say.

Several hours passed between the nurses coming in the room to perform their tasks and the dawn of the next day. I got out of the bed and returned to the chair with Lecia still asleep when one of the nurses came in the room to hang another bag of blood.

She was also given several bags of intravenous fluids to continue to flush the toxins out of her system, and her breasts became engorged when a baby on the television began crying. Milk stains appeared on the third gown they had placed on her. I turned down the sound and a nurse who was assigned to manually express her milk, did her task without even a whimper from Lecia.

She came back later and told me that the third sample results showed that the fluid was clear of drugs.

"Lecia's breast milk is safe for consumption by the baby." Lecia opened her eyes and was awake while the nurse washed her, but she said nothing.

"This is a good sign. She seems more alert today."

"Hi sweetheart." She looked in my direction but remained mute.

Dana and my parents called to check on us, and I told them that she was less lethargic but quiet. The sun was starting to set on another day and the door opened as I was about to hang up the phone. It was my stately maternal grandmother, Barbara Olivia Rogers, bearing her weight on her carved wooden cane.

Michele Sims

CHAPTER TEN

"I couldn't stay away any longer. I needed to see Lecia for myself."

My grandmother, Barbara, the spiritual rock of our family, walked through the doorway and came to the bedside to hug me before she turned and looked at Lecia curled in a tight ball in the bed. She stood there quietly with pain in her soulful brown eyes as she surveyed Lecia, from the top of her hair, spread out and unruly on the pillow, to her knees, as her feet were curled up under her. As if she was a savior commanding a modern-day Lazarus, she opened her mouth with a firm, steady command, bidding Lecia to come forth.

"Open your eyes Lecia." Her head moved slightly, and silent tears formed in the corners of her eyes and fell softly on the pillow.

"It's me, Grammie Mommy, Lecia. I'm here to see about you and pray for you."

Grandma Barbara had taken to referring to herself as Grammie Mommy after Vincent's children appropriately named her that, as she was the mother of their grandmother and my mother, Lauren Vivienne. Lecia opened her eyes and Grammie Mommy reached into her pocket and drew out a small plastic-enclosed container of tissues and handed it to Lecia.

"Thank You, Grammie Mommy." Lecia spoke and cried in her strong embrace. Grammie was a great hugger, and even if only for a moment, she could hug the pain out of you. I went on several visitations with her as a child to offer prayer and comfort to those suffering and in need of strength, so I was familiar with her healing process. I stood, took Lecia's hand, and grabbed my grandmother, who offered a prayer with her usual fervency in our small prayer circle. I found the strength I needed to withstand this current challenge to my faith in God and mankind.

"I know you're in pain and nothing right now can take away the pain of not having your baby you carried in your womb, strengthened with the might of your blood and covered with love, but I wanted to tell you, I'm here for both of you." Lecia leaned into her bosom and cried a little harder, but the feeling of desperation seemed to have lessened.

Grammie did something I hadn't seen her do before in one of her healing ceremonies. She placed her cane to the side and laid her hands on Lecia's face, then gazed without blinking into Lecia's eyes. She cradled Lecia's head with one hand and rubbed her belly in a circular motion with the other and leaned in to kiss Lecia's abdomen through her gown while she firmly kept her hands on the sides of her abdomen. She stretched her neck to look at the ceiling above us and breathed in and out deeply, as if summoning the breath of new life. She grabbed for her cane and walked slowly over to me and, without a smile, took my face into her hands and looked into my eyes. She kissed me on the forehead and said nothing for a few moments until the word "Amen" came out of her mouth.

She positioned her cane in her hand and caressed Lecia's hair. My grandmother had always been a source of support and faith for me. I never questioned her ways even if I poorly understood them.

"I love you Grandma. Thanks for being there for us."

Act I. The Seed on FIre

"I love you too Cade. Of course, I'm here for you. Where else would I be? We'll get through this as a family." She took my chin and surveyed my face.

"You look like you could use a break son. Why don't you go downstairs and get a cup of coffee while I stay here and visit with Lecia? She hasn't said much, and maybe if it's just the two of us, I can get her to speak to me. You know Lecia and I can spend hours talking about the least little things."

"Thanks Grammie, but I'm alright."

"I'm not hearing it. Go sit outside in that nice garden they have across the street and see a little of the sun before it sets. Go."

"Are you sure?" I asked one last time before being pushed out the door.

"Go." She took a seat by the bed and started talking to Lecia while I grabbed my jacket.

I had to admit that it did feel good having a chance to get outside. I wasn't sure if my body hurt from sitting for hours in the same chair or if my muscles were sore because they had tightened from stress. I took the elevator downstairs, and the corridors leading outside were quieter and not as chaotic as the night Lecia was brought into the hospital. I veered to the right to go to the exit, and out of the corner of my eyes, saw a man look at me, then avert his gaze. He was seated off to the side in the back of the room; his jacket was closed with the collar pulled up and he had on dark glasses. If this was 5th Avenue, where stars or people of considerable means were often spotted with their fashionable shades, it wouldn't have caught my attention as odd that he was inside and the only one of about thirty people wearing glasses and avoiding eye contact. He fidgeted as I got closer and stood up, revealing he was Mario's height and build. Could he be here getting my baby checked out? Or maybe his intention was to get to Lecia. I wasn't sure, but I was about the find out.

I kept walking toward him, and the closer I got, the more he seemed to be trying to make a run for the door. I picked up my pace, but hospital orderlies pushing large metal carts filled with supplies blocked path and aided in the man's escape.

"Hey buddy, watch out!" they yelled at me as I almost caused a collision of the carts trying to get past them. I ran to the door and looked both ways before I spotted him trying to cross the street to the park. I sprinted as fast as I could, aided by anger and adrenaline. He started running, and two policeman and a hospital security guard joined in the chase across the busy street, cutting through the park and down a blind alleyway before tackling him as he was scaling the fence at the end of the darkened space. I was out of breath as I came upon the scene just as they were placing him in handcuffs.

"Officers wait, I think I know this man, and he may be wanted in a crime." Stopping to catch my breath, I bent over and placed my hands on my thighs before proceeding. I needed to see his eyes. God help me, if this was Mario, I was going to fuck him up and gladly go to jail for it. I went forward, and his glasses were askew, but still on his face, held there by a black elastic band around the back of his head. I pulled his glasses off and he snarled at me.

"Was it your sister this man assaulted?" one of the officers asked me.

I shook my head, still trying to catch my breath.

"There's a warrant for his arrest, and we got information that he was somewhere in the hospital trying to get to the woman."

"Get off me you bastards!" he yelled at the officers as they finished cuffing him and were dragging him to his feet.

"So, are you just a good Samaritan?" the other officer asked.

"Just a case of mistaken identity," I answered as the man continued to hiss at me.

"Well, there's a reward leading to his arrest and I think you deserve it."

"Give it to charity," I told them as I walked away.

"No good deed goes unpunished," the man yelled at me as they led him away.

You don't know the half of it. The pain of heartache returned as I walked back to the hospital to join Lecia in our private hell.

I tried getting myself together and took my time, first stopping by the bathroom, then going to the cafeteria to get a cup of coffee before returning to the room.

I pushed open the door and was surprised to see Lecia with a small smile on her face as she shared a joke or something with my grandmother.

They both looked at me, and it was my grandmother who spoke.

"See, I told you the sunset was going to be gorgeous tonight. You were gone awhile. Was it nice?"

"Yes, Grammie, it was worth seeing."

I went to the side of the bed and Lecia looked up at me.

"Cade?" She touched my hand and stared into my eyes. I could feel her tension mounting.

"I wish I had news Lecia, but I don't."

"Okay." The rate of her breathing had picked up, but she settled down, assured I was not about to bring bad news.

"Well, this old woman had better call for the limo, so I can get back to the house. I don't want Dana and Vincent to think I got lost. I'm staying at their home." She started gathering her things and kissed Lecia goodbye.

"Bye Grammie. I'm glad you came." Lecia embraced her and raised her hand goodbye before settling in the bed.

"Bye sweetheart." Lecia closed her eyes and a smile rested comfortably on her face as she fell back asleep, probably tired from the extended visit.

You take care of each other Cade, and I'll be back tomorrow."

"Thanks for everything Grams. Let me walk you downstairs." I leaned in to hug her and to plant a kiss on her cheek.

"Don't worry about me. You stay here with Lecia."

"I think she's already asleep." I looked back at Lecia and gave my grandmother my arm to accompany her downstairs. We had reached the door of the suite when Vincent came walking in cradling a blue blanket. He handed his bundle to me and my heart was beating so hard, I thought I was going to pass out. My grandmother looked at Vincent and placed a hand on my shoulder as he gave the baby to me. He supported my arms as I shook slightly after receiving the tiny bundle. My grandmother dropped her cane, placed an arm around my shoulder and her other hand on the baby's head.

"All praises to our heavenly father!" My grandmother smiled and bowed her head. I looked back at Lecia still asleep, wearing a peaceful smile.

The joy of our reunion was broken by several medical professionals who were bursting into the room, wheeling in an incubator and a pediatric crash cart. One of the doctors extended his hand to take my son out of my arms while the walled partition in the room was pushed back by staff members rushing around us.

"We'll be right over there." The doctor told me and pointed to the adjoining space.

"I understand you and your wife were traumatized by his kidnapping and the emotional support team conferred with us so that we would be prepared to avoid any unneeded separations between you and the baby during your stay here. We know he needs to bond with his mother, but right now we need to examine the baby to make sure he's ok. Please may I have him now? I'm sympathetic to your feelings after this traumatic experience, and I also know that any of those guards outside the door will shoot me if I attempted to leave with this baby. You can come over to the examination area with me, but I ask you to put on a protective mask and gown, and I need you to promise to stay out of the way."

There was no time to communicate with Lecia, who somehow had fallen into a deep sleep despite the commotion going on around us.

"Go with them," Vincent demanded. "Grammie and I will stay over here with Lecia. I need Gram's assistance anyway."

I handed over my son and walked the short distance to be with him while they examined him. The partition was pulled back, separating me from Lecia, and a nurse came to me and put forms in my face to sign, consenting to care for my son and to having samples taken from the baby. I reviewed the forms as fast as I could and signed them.

The staff assisted me in the antiseptic washing of my hands, gowning, and gloving procedure and I was amazed at the symphony of movement around me. Each member of the team knew their role and acted in concert with each other. My boy was sleeping on his back while he was examined by the lead pediatrician. He squirmed as he was disturbed from his rest by a small needle placed in his heel. I noticed we had the same birthmark on our right great toe, and he let out a scream, revealing his brown eyes with green flecks and the soft pinkness of the back of his throat.

Sorry my boy, the fun is just starting. Suddenly, I had the baby yelling in front of me and Lecia calling out to me on the other side of the partition.

"Cade is that my baby?" I sensed the frenzy building in her voice. Vincent and Grammie began yelling at me too.

"Answer her Cade or we'll have to restrain her to stop her from getting out of bed." They yelled to me.

"Yes Lecia. He's our son." I was laughing; and tears of joy started filling my mask. The doctor took his stethoscope and tried to warm it up before placing it on my son's chest and I jumped as the baby let out a yell like a banshee. The doctor removed his diaper and we both saw he had been circumcised. I couldn't remember when I lost my foreskin, but I realized the procedure must have been painful for my little one. After the team finally finished assessing him, washing him and covering his tender appendage, one of the nurses handed him to me, and this time I was more comfortable having my boy in my arms. I embraced him, kissed him on the forehead and started singing a soft soothing tune.

"Can I take him to his mother?" I turned to ask the doctor.

"Please do. I'm sure she's anxious to hold her baby." He pulled back the partition to allow Lecia an unobstructed view of our child. She stretched her arms to us with tears in her eyes and, with a sense of urgency, bade me to come to her.

"Bring the baby to me Cade. I want to see our child."

These were the first complete sentences she had been able to form since being poisoned with a cocktail of drugs.

I looked at her and noticed her gown had been changed again, but this time the new gown had a flap on it to allow for breastfeeding. I walked over to her and placed our son in her arms. She drew him to her chest and he began rooting to try to find a nipple for nourishment and comfort. I watched as she used the privacy flap to expose just enough of her breast to allow our boy to suckle. He took the breast in his mouth and Lecia positioned him so that he fed in the comfort of her arms.

"Hello my sweet boy. I'm your mommy."

I could tell she wanted to examine him, but she delayed her mommy exam until he finished feeding. I went to the side opposite the breast where my son was feeding, sat on the bed and embraced my family. I didn't need a blood test to prove what I already knew in my heart. I choked on the lump in my throat as I watched in appreciation that my precious child had been returned to us. I was also struck by the pure simplicity of the moment. Lecia looked up at me and offered me a kiss before quickly turning her bright beaming smile back to our son, mixed with a look of pride and insatiable longing that she wouldn't ever get enough of holding him. I looked at Vincent and Grammie observing the scene of mother and child, and my grandmother was wiping away her tears with her handkerchief.

"Vincent do you think they fed him?" I asked my brother, looking at how enthusiastically he was pulling on his mother's breast.

"Yes, he was being fed. That's how we found him."

Lecia had not verbalized that she recalled what had happened to her, and she didn't look up or join in the conversation. She was too absorbed in the moment.

"My understanding is he ate so much of the food stored in the room for him that it was threatening their supply. The concierge called my team after he received a request for a case of formula to be delivered to the room where the baby was being watched by the babysitter. He told me he heard an infant screaming in the background and he recorded some of the call. I listened to the recording and the baby sounded so much like Aria as an infant. I recognized the demanding nature of his yell and I knew he had to be your kid. Well, the truth is I was praying he was your baby." I laughed with Vincent like I had never laughed before. "The babysitter offered very little resistance after we explained the situation, and she didn't want to be charged as an accomplice."

"I've always told you I had an appreciation for Aria's temperament, and I knew she had it for a reason. I didn't know understanding and appreciating her temperament would be the thing that would save the life of my child and that you would use it to recognize the voice of my son. Thank you, Vincent, for bringing him back to us." Lecia looked up at us with tears in her eyes.

"Thanks to both of you. You saved my life." The baby continued his sucking until he wasn't drawing enough from that breast. He started shaking his fists again, loosened his grip on the nipple with a *pop,* and let out a yell of frustration. His face reddened as Lecia positioned him on the other breast and he began sucking again. He finished feeding and passed out in her arms.

"So, you haven't found Mario yet?" Lecia directed her question to Vincent. "I don't remember much at this point, but I remember having to fight him off me."

"No, we haven't yet, but we will. I've promised myself that he'll face justice."

"Just not sure what kind of justice." She looked back and forth between me and Vincent after his veiled declaration of revenge.

"I can see the answer in both of your faces, so I won't ask the hard questions since I may not be prepared to hear the answers. I'll be right back. I need to use the bathroom." Lecia pushed the call bell to get assistance and gave the baby to me before walking to the bathroom with help from one of the nurses. I was cradling the baby when the door opened, and the four Moore children, Dana, Dad, and Mom spilled into the room.

"We couldn't stay away any longer," Mom told me.

They all knew the routine. Everyone had to wash their hands before touching the baby. Lecia had rehearsed the routine with them as she'd gotten closer to the end of her pregnancy. They all placed foam on their hands and rubbed the foam away. Lecia was in the bathroom when the family burst out into laughter.

"What's so funny?" she called out.

"Are you alright? Come and see for yourself," I called.

"I'm still a little weak. Hello everybody." She came back into the room and was surprised by the additional visitors as she took slow small steps with the nurses assisting her back to the bed. The baby was sprawled out in my arms with what appeared to be a smile on his face. His eyes were closed, and he was asleep as she looked at him and smiled.

"That's just gas, Cade," she commented about his sweet smile.

"Probably, but does he remind you of anyone? Everyone here thought he looked like you." The family started laughing again.

"Is that how I look when I'm asleep?" Lecia asked while I beamed with pride and delight as I looked at my boy.

"This is exactly how you look when you're asleep and satisfied." She rolled her eyes at me, having received my message on several intended levels.

"Can you lay the baby on his back after I get situated in bed?"

I knew she wanted to examine him since she was his mother and a nurse practitioner. She looked at his fingers, his toes, and rubbed a finger along the soft skin on his cheeks with two of the younger children on each side of the bed. She checked his knees and ankles, slowly extending his joints. She took off his little t-shirt and rubbed her fingers down his spine and opened his diaper to the air to see his Moore's male birthright. She was careful in touching him, as he was still sore. He whimpered and opened his eyes for a few seconds.

Alex thought the baby looked like him and my father, while Lexie thought the baby looked like her and her daddy, Vincent. The twins had their own opinions.

"The baby looks like me and Austin but with my eyes," Aria declared, and Austin nodded in agreement while their parents and grandparents looked on but didn't declare their opinions. It was a good thing each family member saw a bit of themselves in my boy. I looked at Lecia, who was busy covering the baby in his blanket.

"So, who do you think the baby looks like?" It didn't take her long to respond.

"He has the look of love and grace." She closed his diaper and took him back into her arms. *Burp.* The family started laughing again. I couldn't put into words how happy I was to have my son back with his family. Dad asked the question I thought others were dying to ask.

"Are we going to call him "the baby" for the rest of his life? What are you going to name him?"

I looked at Lecia and she looked at my grandmother.

"I would like Grammie Mommy's opinion." She cradled the baby and looked toward my grandmother.

"Well, I think the name should honor the spirit of this little one. He was the only one who had to fight to return to this family, and he had to travel in peril. He was born on the night of his father's greatest professional triumph to date, and Alex told me that his uncle Cade was trading last night on that machine he has, his computer. He said that was a good thing."

I gathered the children had been told a little of what happened to Lecia and our son since none asked why Gram was saying he had to fight to be with the family.

"No Grammie Mommy. Uncle Cade was trending, not trading on the computer," Alex reminded her.

"Cade doesn't want the baby named for him," Lecia added.

"The baby will bear the name of his great-grandfather, Aaron Moore, his grandfather, Charles Aiden Moore and his father, Kaiden Moore by bearing their last name, Baby Boy Moore. Lecia, you told me your father traveled many miles from El Salvador, to the Dominican Republic to get to this country and Miles Davis is Kaiden's favorite musician. I think it is obvious that we name the baby, Miles Aridio Tavares Moore."

I looked at Lecia and smiled.

"I like the name, Lecia."

"I agree, but with two conditions. I want Grammie Mommy to perform his christening and Vincent and Dana to be Miles' godparents."

"It would be my honor to perform the christening ceremony." She smiled as if it were Christmas morn. A new baby had come to the family and she was grateful we had something to celebrate.

"We would consider it an honor to be his godparents." Vincent and Dana looked at each other and then at us.

The children were excited to be god-siblings as well as cousins to Miles. Dana was like an older sister to Lecia, and they had developed a close relationship in a short period of time. Aria was about to climb up on the bed when Dana tried grabbing her.

"No Aria. You can't get up there while the baby is on the bed. Remember you're a big girl now."

"I know that, Mommy. The baby is in Tia Lecia's arms and I was getting on the bed to help her. I have my papers."

"Aria, what am I saying to you?" Dana made direct eye contact with her and responded in her *you're trying mommy* voice.

"You told me not to get on the bed, but Mommy please listen to me. I have my papers," she replied and scampered to get her green backpack. She unzipped her bag, pulled out a rolled-up piece of paper and gave it to her mother.

"Daddy told me if I was willing to work hard, good things will come my way."

Dana looked down at the paper and began reading it out loud.

"This is to certify that Marie Ariadne Moore has completed her training as an assistant to Tia Lecia and she will help in caring for the new baby. Aria can wash her hands, put on her gloves, and use diaper wipes to assist in cleaning the baby if she so desires. She can answer the phone to tell others that Tia Lecia is caring for the baby, tell them to please call back, and she knows how to dial 911 if instructed to by Tia Lecia." Dana looked at her daughter and then at Lecia.

"She did work hard, and she is certified," Lecia told her. Aria took a little apron out of her backpack that had "Tia's Little Helper" embroidered on the bib. She took off her shoes and this time asked if she could get on the bed.

"I could use the help, Dana. Aria, can you get a diaper and the wipes for me? Your uncle Cade will show you where they are, and maybe you can help teach your uncle Cade how to change a diaper."

I directed Aria to the location where the diapers and the wipes were kept. This time she looked at her mother before crawling onto the bed. Vincent was exhausted and asleep in the chair, with Lexie curled up in his arms while he slept. I hoped I would be as good a father to Miles as Vincent was to his children. I loved my brother, and it was true I envied and admired him at the same time, but it was always the love overriding any other emotion that kept our relationship strong. I turned my head back to the bed and looked on as Aria with her gloved hand demonstrated her skills in giving the wipes to Lecia with the same precision as a surgical nurse. She then gave her the diaper and pulled out a small plastic bag. She also knew to hold the plastic bag wide open while Lecia deposited the soiled diaper in it. Aria removed her gloves, placed them in the bag, and got off the bed to throw it away. They completed their task before Miles began placing his little fists in his mouth, showing he wanted to feed again. He was smacking his lips and moving his head in search of a nipple.

My mother was uncharacteristically quiet for a family gathering, and so was my father. I sensed they both preferred to be quiet and enjoy the time observing the new baby, as I had seen them do the same thing after the birth of each of

Vincent's children. Dana started telling the kids to gather their things so that Lecia and the baby could have some private time.

"That's our cue to leave so you can feed Miles in peace." She went over to kiss Vincent and wake him up.

"Vincent, we need to go home so you can get some rest. Tell Uncle Cade and Aunt Lecia goodbye," she told her children.

"That sounds like a good idea. Oh, by the way, I had your apartment cleaned so you won't have to go home to a mess." Vincent spoke, stifling a yawn at the same time.

"Thanks bro. I appreciate that."

"I'll leave with them too," Grandma Barbara told us.

I saw Lecia getting a little weepy. She was the happiest I had seen her in days, and it occurred to me she felt safer surrounded by the family.

"Don't cry Tia Lecia," the children took turns reassuring her. "We'll be back to see you and Miles tomorrow."

Aria piped in, "Miles will be ok. Grammie Mommy and the rest of us prayed for him."

I didn't know how that little girl was able to read Lecia's feelings, but I saw Lecia calming with Aria's compassion.

"Cade, can you get the small bottle of breast milk out of the refrigerator and warm it up for me? The nurses told me they were storing my milk." She had expressed the milk earlier with the assistance of one of the nurses, and I smiled, understanding she was giving me my turn to feed Miles.

They all gave us a hug before leaving and my parents were preparing to leave when the door opened, and it was Marisela pushing Aridio in his wheelchair and my sister in law Marissa.

On my way to the kitchenette to prepare a bottle, I stopped and hugged each member of the Tavares family. Lecia looked up, surprised to see her family.

"Papi, Mami, and Marissa. I'm so happy to see all of you."

"The baby and Lecia are waiting to see all of you, and Papi, there's a special surprise. Would you like to see your new grandson and namesake?" I asked.

Papi and Mami covered their mouths, surprised by the fact Miles had been named for him. They walked over to the bedside where Lecia was sitting up holding him and they cleaned their hands with the wipes before reaching the bedside. Papi and Mami said hello to my parents but kept their eyes on their new grandson. His eyes were closed when I left the bedside and he opened them in a hunger protest.

"He has a little bit of green in his eyes just like Aria and Dana. Cade are you ready to bring the bottle?" Papi asked.

My father looked at me fumbling with the bottle as Miles became more insistent in his demands, and he thankfully distracted them with conversation.

"He has flecks of green in his eyes, which was the color of my mother's eyes. She was a beautiful woman of Irish and English descent, with clear green eyes, and Cade passed the genes to his son. I see some of the Tavares genes in him too, with his thick head of brown hair. I wish we could stay longer, but we need to be going. It was good seeing you again, and I'm sure you'll enjoy your time with the baby. Please have my seat, Marisela, and both of you enjoy our grandson, Miles Aridio Moore."

"We want to thank you and Lauren for letting us know the baby was here. I couldn't stand the thought that our first grandson was in the world and I wasn't here to welcome him." Papi extended his hand to my parents.

"Yes, thank you. It was a challenge getting here, but with Marissa's help we made it and it was certainly worth the effort."

My parents accepted their acknowledgment of gratitude and left after saying goodbye.

I wiped away the sweat from my brow and waved goodbye to my parents before returning to the bedside. My nerves were frayed from hearing someone so little scream at the top of his lungs. Lecia had her hands outstretched to give him to me. I quickly placed the bottle in his mouth then placed him with his bottle in the arms of his abuela for the first time.

He stopped yelling and settled in Marisela's arms, once again surrounded by the love and attention of his family. I sat back on the bed with Lecia, who was giggling at me.

"Are you alright Daddy Cade? You looked like you were on the verge of a heart attack."

"That boy knows how to yell—and in key. He'll make a good singer one day."

She smiled, and a nurse came in to detach her from the IV.

"You won't be needing this anymore," she informed her.

Her sister Marissa was quiet and looked intently at Lecia's face, still covered with blue marks on the side of her face and cheek from her encounter with Mario.

"Lecia, what happened to your face?" Marissa looked at her with concern and turned Lecia's chin, so she could look closer at her.

"I fell, Marissa, just before I went into labor." She looked at Marissa and, for a few moments, no words passed between them.

"No, Marissa, Cade and I were not involved in a struggle. We don't fight like that."

My head snapped in the direction of the two women together on the bed. Lecia did look like a battered woman, and I guess it didn't register before because my family said nothing about it. They knew the truth of what had happened to her, though we didn't tell my parents that Mario was responsible for it. Her family knew nothing of the ordeal, but to blame me? *What the hell.* Her parents were looking at me too, but it was Marissa who echoed their concerns while grabbing a hold to Lecia's hand.

"We have a pact with each other Lecia. I love Cade like a brother, but we've agreed that if we see something that doesn't look or feel right, we'll say something even if it's painful for the other to hear. That's why I'm asking you in front of Cade. I don't want to accuse him of something falsely and hold concerns about him in my heart." I cleared my throat and felt I needed to say something.

"Marissa I would never raise my hand to my wife, and I promise you I'd kill any man who felt he could get away with assaulting her." My face heated in fury and I was breathing so deeply, my chest heaved with anger.

"Cade, I'm sorry I brought it up, but I needed to know. I love my sister and I think highly of you. It was hard for me to mention it, but I felt I had to ask." I calmed down, knowing I needed to reign in my temper, which seemed to confuse them even more. It wasn't lost on me that even Papi had leaned back and away from me in response to my reaction to Marissa's question.

"Marissa you know I wouldn't stay with a man who abused me." Lecia tried to reassure her.

"But Lecia, what about Daniella who—"

145

"Marissa, that's enough. Lecia has already told you Cade didn't abuse her and why would you want to risk poisoning our relationship with him by continuing this line of questioning?" Aridio turned to me.

"Cade, you've been good to us, especially during my recovery, and I hope you weren't offended but, I agree with Marissa that the question had to be raised even if the timing was awkward."

"No offense taken. I've been so concerned about Lecia and the baby; I guess I wasn't as focused on the bruising still on her face. I also should have called you myself to let you know what was going on and I ask your forgiveness for that."

"Your parents called and let us know you hadn't left Lecia's side and for that we are grateful," Marisela added, and Miles stirred, diverting everyone's attention. "My grandson is so beautiful." She looked at him and beamed with pride.

I saw that fatigue was setting in and Lecia was smiling but yawning and fighting sleep at the same time. Her family stayed for about twenty minutes more and we insisted they spend the night at our apartment while I slept at the hospital with Lecia and Miles. They prepared to leave, and it took Mami a little longer than Papi to separate from Lecia and the baby.

"Lecia, you look tired and need your rest. We'll see you later," Marisela conceded.

"We're good Cade?" Marissa asked me.

"Always sister. I know you and Lecia have always had each other's back." I accepted her embrace.

"We should be leaving, but Cade, can I speak to you at the door?" Papi asked.

"Sure. Lecia, I'll be back." I got behind his chair and pushed him to the hall outside the door while the women said their final goodbyes.

"How can I help Papi?"

"I had one question. Why are these guards stationed outside the door?"

"There was an earlier foiled abduction of an infant and we wanted the added protection to keep Lecia and Miles safe." I failed to tell them the infant was Miles.

"You can't be too careful when it comes to your children." He patted me on the hand.

"We'll be back to visit you tomorrow. Do you think Lecia will be released tomorrow?" He asked me.

"I hope she and the baby are released tomorrow, but the doctors haven't given us a release date yet." We hugged and said our goodbyes after Marisela and Marissa joined us in the hall. I returned to Lecia, who was turned on her side, yawning and fighting sleep while Miles was propped up in her arms and sucking at her breast. I waited until he finished to burp him and placed him in his bassinette beside us, pulling it close to Lecia so she could see him the moment she opened her eyes.

We got a little rest, but three hours later Miles was back at it again. Although the kid had a healthy appetite, Lecia never complained. She was so happy having our son in her arms.

It felt right in our world again as I looked at them before going to the bathroom. To my surprise, he was in his bassinette asleep instead of nursing when I returned.

"He wasn't hungry. He just needed to be held and get some reassurance we were still here. Look at our son Cade, he's so perfect!" Tears welled up and she took her lower lip in her mouth.

"Why are you crying Lecia?"

"I almost lost my perfect gift second only to the gift of marrying you. He's so beautiful and I fought for him Cade. I promise I did and I'm so sorry what Miles had to go through."

"I never doubted you fought for our son Lecia, and there's videotape to prove it."

"What videotape?" Lecia frowned I hoped more from curiosity than irritation.

"Vincent had a security system install in the front of our apartment and believe me, you put up a fight. Lecia, I don't blame you for what happened to you and Miles. Our baby is beautiful, safe, and you not only protected him, but you grew him in your body and I'm grateful to you for giving me the perfect son."

"Thank you, but maybe I blame myself for not seeing Mario for who he is."

"We'll talk about Mario later. My focus is on us healing as a family."

"Yes, you're right, and sorry for not coming to your defense with my family. I saw how angry you were at being accused of hurting me." I sighed as she muffled a yawn.

"You've been apologizing since you gave birth. Lecia, let's not continue to do this to each other—you apologize and me saying over and over I don't blame you. Us being together as a family again is what's important." I took her into my arms and settled down for another night in the hospital.

"I agree if you promise to stop comparing yourself to your brother. I can tell that's a sore point for you, and it may get worse if you compare how you parent Miles to how he chooses to parent his children."

"Oh, so you're wanting to go there now? You didn't have to grow up in Vincent's shadow." I asserted.

"He's seven years older than you; don't you think he should have been stronger and more experienced than you growing up? But oh, I forgot how competitive you Moores' can be."

"Yes, competitive even when the odds are against us, but I know you're talking about my family with all the love you can muster." I kept her close in my arms and started yawning too.

"You know I love your family, but I'm crazy in love with you. You're my Superhombre."

"Your Superhombre, you say? What super powers do I have?" She giggled as I pinched her on her butt cheek.

"Well, you give the best hugs, and I feel so loved and protected in your arms. You love with your whole heart, and you're willing to sacrifice for me and the baby. You've made me feel like I'm the luckiest woman in the world and you're all mine."

"Alright, I promise to at least be aware of how often I compare myself to him, especially since I've already won the grand prize. I have your love."

"Uh huh, my love..." she yawned once more and fell asleep in my arms.

Michele Sims

CHAPTER ELEVEN

Lecia was regaining her strength and each day was better for her than the day before. She was more alert and required less assistance from the nurses while little Miles was turning into a well-tuned eating and pooping machine. He had two consecutive days of gaining more weight in ounces, and his demand for his mother's milk seemed endless. Lecia reveled at each time he cried for her and cuddled him with love and patience as he nursed.

"So, do you think the three of you are ready to go home?" The doctor came into the room and surprised us with his recommendations that we were ready. I could hardly contain my joy, and Lecia bounced on the bed with excitement.

"We can go today?" we asked as if repeating a chorus to a familiar song.

"As soon we get the paperwork done." He patted her on the shoulder and told us the nurses would give us information for care at home and our follow-up schedule.

"I trust your training and experience as a nurse practitioner will serve you well, and I think you all have bonded well as the parents of a newborn. Take care, and I'll see you at your follow-up." He turned and left the room while she sprang into action to get dressed before dressing Miles for his first trip home.

"What do you want me to do?"

"Call the family and tell them to meet us at home this evening since we'll be back at the apartment."

She did a little dance and scurried around the room collecting our things as fast as she could.

I walked up to the door burdened like a pack mule with baby stuff and Lecia's suitcase while she carried the baby.

"I hope you like it." I told her at the hospital that I had authorized a few changes during the renovations. I held my breath as I struggled to place the key in the door and opened it very slowly for dramatic effect. I had Mami leave the lights on so Lecia could see the new décor as I moved out the way and allowed her the first full view of our interior design. She opened her mouth and stood in the doorway until I nudged her to step inside.

"Oh Cade. Oh my gosh. I love it." She brought the baby inside the room, which had been painted a silver gray, accented in white trim. The design was sleek and contemporary with a new gray couch and baby-blue accents.

"Welcome home Lecia and Miles." She rocked the baby lightly in her arms as she looked around. The curtain panels were pulled back, and sun streamed in, framing the stylish New York skyline. She turned in a full circle, taking in the changes.

"I thought changing this room in light of what happened would be good for all of us."

"Cade, I agree." Her eyes misted as she sat on the new couch and shivered from an imagined draft in the room. She drew the baby closer to her breast and held him tight. He stirred but was settling back to sleep in her arms before I pulled the small bassinette out into the room and urged her to put him down while she finished her walk through the apartment.

"I don't want to leave him out here alone." We looked up as her father wheeled himself into the room.

"You are home and you've brought the bambino with you." He wheeled closer to the bassinette where Miles was placed in his new baby-blue outfit.

"Where's Mami and Marissa?" Lecia asked as she held on to the baby.

"They went out shopping for a few things."

"Please don't tell me they went out to buy baby things. I told Mami, Miles had everything he needed."

"He has everything except something from his grandparents, and she couldn't accept that we were asked not to give him anything." Lecia shrugged and conceded the point.

"Lecia, why don't you let Papi visit with Miles while I show you the rest of the house?" I gathered most of her things in one hand and grabbed her by the hand.

"They'll be fine, and we won't be far. The place is bigger—but not that big." I was able to coach a smile out of her and she agreed to continue the walkthrough. We walked down the hall to our bedroom and I opened the door. There were fewer changes made to this space, and this time she held her breath as I opened the door and let out her breath after walking into the room.

"Thank goodness, you kept the bed. I love our four-post cherry wood bed. It's so traditional."

"Yes, I love the bed too; some of my happiest memories were made there. I got rid of the mattress, but the frame of the bed is the same. I made love to you for the first time in this bed, and my son was conceived there. I didn't want to part with it." I took her into my arms, now free of stuff, and placed a kiss on her lips.

"While we're talking about beds, I need to tell you I plan to sleep with Miles in his room."

I started shaking my head.

"No Lecia. I don't see that happening. No, final answer."

"Let me explain." I continued to shake my head. "Cade, if I sleep with Miles, we won't wake you up after midnight and you can go back to your work schedule. You know your compositions suffer when you're sleep deprived, and it will just be a matter of time before your performance suffers if you're only getting three to four hours of sleep. If I'm back and forth checking on the baby, I'll disturb you."

"You'll sleep in the bed with me and we'll keep Miles in this bedroom until the two of you get settled in. You're my wife and we should sleep together. I don't think I'm asking too much, and I don't care to discuss this anymore." I rubbed my hand through my hair.

"How do you like the space? You haven't seen the bathroom." I redirected her to the bathroom and she looked in at the new cabinets, marble tops, and gleaming silver fixtures.

"I love it Cade. You've been so thoughtful and patient with me. I'll return to bed with you for now and we can discuss our sleeping arrangements for the next few weeks later. I think I hear the baby." She turned and walked away.

"Let's go check on him and Aridio." There was no need to urge her to go back to him as she was already making a beeline to get Miles. Aridio looked up at us and around the room as if he needed to be assured of privacy before he spoke. We took a seat on the couch and Lecia held on to the baby.

"While I have the chance, I need to share something with the two of you. I've struggled with how to tell you this, but I need to get it off my chest. First, I need to warn you about Mario. I had a chance to look over the books, and some money was missing. I help his mother manage her share of the company, even though I bought out most of her shares before her husband died. He asked me on his deathbed to look out for Lydia and the boys, but I think as I was so distracted by the upcoming birth of the baby and then the accident, that Mario used it as his chance to steal funds from the company. Antonio also confirmed my suspicions."

"Papi, I thought things weren't adding up too after I reviewed some of the books, but I didn't want to burden you with additional worries. I wanted you to concentrate on getting better, and I don't think he stole more than twenty-five thousand dollars."

"Well, he tried to steal more and was in the process of shifting money into his personal accounts when Antonio stopped him from taking the funds by authorizing a freeze on all my accounts until I or my representative could review the books. I think Mario is out for revenge, so I want you to be aware he may pose a risk of danger to the family including you, Cade, and the baby."

"Aridio, there's something we need to tell you." I shifted my body to face him.

"Cade, not now. Let's wait until Papi is better." Lecia touched my leg and squirmed in her seat. She managed to silence me, but it didn't stop Papi from releasing whatever was still on his mind.

"Lecia, let me finish. There's more. Lydia and I had an encounter one night before she married Rafael."

"What do you mean by an encounter Papi?" He looked down at his hands and moved the leg still in a cast that was elevated on the brace of his wheelchair.

"I'm ashamed of my actions, but Lydia and I got drunk after a set at the club, and it's possible I'm Mario's father." Lecia stopped rocking the baby and placed him back in the bassinette while she and her father decided when they could look at each other. I grabbed her hand for support.

"Somehow, Mario found out from Lydia's meddling sister about my brief relationship with Lydia before I married your mother. He's an angry young man, Lecia, and he's angry with his father for leaving him and angry with me for never claiming him as possibly being my son." Lecia looked down at our hands joined together on the couch and I decided it was time to come clean about Mario's attack on Lecia.

"While we're being honest, I need to tell you the truth surrounding Miles' birth. The reason Lecia delivered early was because Mario and an accomplice induced her into labor with drugs and then kidnapped the baby. My brother and a few of his friends in law enforcement located Miles and returned him to us." I swore all the blood drained out of his face and he looked ashen and close to collapse. Lecia looked up at her father whose breathing was fast and shallow.

"Breathe Papi. Place your head down and take in a breath." She was talking to him when the door opened, and her mother walked in the front room, carrying a silk box with a blue satin bow tied on top.

"Lecia and Cade, you're home!" She was on her way to look at Miles who was sleeping in his bassinette. She grabbed his little hand as she bent over him and smiled. She looked to the side and her countenance immediately changed.

"Aridio, you don't look well. What's going on? Should I call your doctor? Lecia, what do you think is wrong with him?" He calmed his breathing and responded to her.

"I'll be alright. I got overexcited looking at my beautiful grandson—our nieto."

"Yes, our nieto. We've lived long enough to see our first grandson. I'm so happy, I'm drawn to tears every time I think about." She sat on the couch and placed the box on her lap.

"Where's Marissa, Mami?"

"She's visiting with our cousins. She wanted to see the family before we returned to North Carolina."

"Is that the present you bought for Lecia? I told her you were out shopping?"

"Si, si. It's for Miles. It's sentimental and not new. I hope you and Cade like it." Lecia took the box and untied the blue bow as we looked on in anticipation and gasped after she pulled back the light blue tissue paper.

"I had your christening gown, the smaller one, and Miguel's gown cleaned and restored. The hat and booties belonged to Miguel. If you approve, I thought Miles could wear one of the outfits at his christening." I looked over her shoulder at the white silk gown with a panel of lace running down the center of the skirt. Lecia bit her bottom lip and struggled to say something. She swallowed hard and a tear dropped down her cheek as she looked at the gowns, which were similar except one had more lace than the other.

"Thank you so much Mami and Papi. I didn't know you still had our christening gowns. I saw pictures of us from that day, but I never saw the gowns."

"We kept them but never opened the box after we left the Dominican Republic until now. I wanted you to have them both. I think either gown will fit him, but the silk hat and booties belonged to your brother Miguel." Mami choked up and looked to Papi for support. He took her outstretched hand in his and kissed the back of her hand.

"I'm glad you brought the gowns. I can't think of a more special gift. I'll dress Miles in the gown today." We all looked at Lecia, uncertain about her decision.

"Call Marissa Mami. Miles will be christened this evening. I'll call Grammie Mommy to remind her of her promise to preside over his christening during her visit here."

"Lecia, we have plenty of food for a family gathering, but don't you think it's too early for a christening? You just got home today."

"Today is as good as any, and I don't want to wait. I want Grammie Mommy to bless Miles today." The baby started stirring and whimpering as if he knew his mother had spoken and her words were final. He placed his little fist in his mouth and started making sucking noises.

"Mommy's got you. It's okay." She got up, took him out of his bassinette and placed him on her chest near her shoulder.

"Mami, please call Marissa and tell her about the christening in the next few hours. I need to go feed and dress Miles. Cade, can you bring his christening outfit to the room when you come?"

"Sure thing." I rose to carry out her orders.

"Lecia, your Papi and I will put out the food. Shall we change into something dressy? We didn't bring many changes of clothes."

"No, that won't be necessary. This will be an event for close family members only: Cade's parents, Vincent, Dana and the kids, Marissa and of course Grammie Mommy."

"As you wish Lecia. I see your mind is made up."

"Yes Mami, it is. I think Papi also has something he wanted to tell you."

I sat on the couch in the center of an emotional landmine that could explode at any time. Her beliefs in her father as the model of integrity had been shattered before she had time to fully ingest the horror of what her childhood friend and possibly her brother had done to her. Lecia was strong, and she would get through this, and I would be there for her the whole way.

She and Miles weren't the only ones who could use a blessing—we all could. It sure wouldn't hurt right now. I got up and took the box with the christening gowns into the bedroom.

Michele Sims

CHAPTER TWELVE

"Why Aridio? How could Mario do such a thing to Lecia and our family? I knew he was an angry young man, but I would have never imagined this."

Marisela had changed her clothes and covered her dress with her favorite apron and was patting her foot and searching Aridio's eyes for answers. Before he could answer, she got up off the couch.

"I have to check on the food. I don't want it to burn." She paced a bit and placed her cupped hand on her neck before heading off to the kitchen to check on the food.

Each time she opened the door to the kitchen, the scents of spicy chicken, beans, rice, sweet-smelling desserts and fruits wafted through the space. I grabbed my stomach to suppress the growls escaping from the hunger pit in my abdomen. Lecia still hadn't come out of the bedroom, which meant I had to navigate the situation and Lecia's parents by myself. I wasn't aware of how much Aridio had told his wife while I was in the bedroom with Lecia, and I prayed I wouldn't spill the beans of Mario's possible paternity.

"Aridio, answer me!" Marisela returned from the kitchen with a large wooden spoon in her hand. Her sadness was turning into anger, and I moved over on the couch away from the love seat where she sat with Aridio to miss any blows not intended for me. This situation was heating up, and I looked to the bedroom, hoping Lecia and Miles would provide reinforcements soon to stop things from boiling over.

"If you sit still, maybe I can explain things to you, Marisela."

I piped in to take some of the pressure off Aridio. "Marisela, there is no explanation for this. His actions were unconscionable." She turned in my direction with her spoon still held high.

"Cade, you're sure Mario—Mario Rodriguez—had something to do with Miles' kidnapping? He was angry with Aridio, but I could never imagine him hurting Lecia. He's always been like a big brother to her. As he entered his teen years, he seemed less invested in maintaining a relationship with us and came to the house less often."

"I'm sure Marisela. We had the apartment under surveillance, and there's videotaped evidence of Mario being here and assaulting Lecia, along with an accomplice."

"He didn't...violate her. Did he?"

"No Aridio, he didn't. He placed her in the bedroom after drugging her and came back seconds later to where he was seen on camera. I'm angry enough to kill him for what he did to us, and if I thought he sexually violated her in addition to the physical assault and kidnapping, we would be talking about the late Mario Rodriguez." Marisela sprang up from her seat again.

"I can't hear any more of this. I need to be with Lecia."

"Please, Marisela. Let her focus on Miles right now. Taking care of him seems to be getting her through this trauma. I only talk about Mario when she brings him up, which isn't frequent, and I don't think she could handle a lot of questions at this time," I pleaded, hoping her parents would understand.

"Alright, I'll let her get through the day, but I can't promise I'll remain silent and not offer my daughter comfort. I'm her mother, and even though she's now a mother, she and Marissa will always be my children." She got up and headed in the direction of the kitchen. She pushed the door open and my stomach started growling again.

"You really need to feed that little monster inside you." She smiled for the first time.

Aridio made sure she was in the kitchen before he spoke again.

"I'll tell her the whole thing about Mario after we get home. I'm aware you and your brother have taken things into your own hands when it comes to protecting your family. Mario has driven a dagger in my heart, and even if he has my blood, he's no longer a son of mine. He has crossed a red line by placing my daughter and grandson in danger. You'll not experience any repercussions from me if you do what you feel you have to do."

"I hear you." We sat quietly together in the knowledge that Mario would be dealt with and how he was dealt with would not be a topic of discussion between us, ever again.

There was a knock at the door, and I got up, thinking my family had arrived for the christening.

It was Marissa who stomped in, red faced and puffed up as if ready for battle.

"What was the emergency? You know I don't get to see Rosita very often and we were planning to hang out and dance the night away. I get summoned by Lecia and I have to come to be with the family as if I never have plans of my own." I ushered her into the front room, where her parents could address her concerns. I had never seen such a reversal of power in the Tavares household. First Lecia, who had difficulty looking at her Papi, then Marisela holding a wooden spoon over his head, and now Marissa, who wasn't about to take direction from her parents. I felt sorry for the man who, for the moment, literally couldn't stand up for himself. He sat in the chair with his leg still elevated and immobilized with metal pins.

"Marissa, you're a part of the family and we were sure you didn't want to miss the celebration and the chance to support your only sister in the whole wide world while she had her first and only child christened. I needed to get back to preparing the food and I didn't have time to tell you about the christening. I was also afraid if I told you, you'd tell Rosita and they'd be offended that they weren't invited." Marisela was facing her youngest offspring with the same spoon held high and menacing in her hand.

"When you put it like that Mami, no, I wouldn't have wanted to miss the celebration. Let me put my things in the room and I'll come help you in the kitchen. Do you think we have enough food?"

"Yes, we have enough, but the meal is a simple one. I wasn't expecting to host a christening either, but if this is what Lecia wants, as her family, we'll support her, yes mija?"

"Of course, Mami. Let me freshen up and I'll be back."

One crisis averted, and the doorbell rang again. I went to the door to answer it and my family started spilling in. The twins ran past me with their mother, Dana, trying to corral them, followed by the two older children and my parents.

"Where's Vincent and Grammie Mommy?"

"They're downstairs, and Vincent stayed behind to help wheel her chair up here. Her arthritis has been acting up. She wanted to get here as soon as possible, and you know how she has to stop and talk to everyone," my mother advised me. "Leave the door ajar and they can come right in. I noticed the building had more security personnel on duty."

"They had better have more security. I'm being charged extra for it." I escorted them into the room where Aridio was sitting. Dana left to help Marisela in the kitchen with the appetizers and returned with a tray of finger foods.

"The meal won't be fancy." Marisela came in the room also carrying a tray.

"Hello Marisela." My mother got up to hug her. "I'm sure everything will be fantastic. You're such a great cook. What can I do to help?"

"Thank you, Lauren, but I've got it under control. Where's your mother?"

"She and Vincent are on their way up now." Vincent wheeled Grammie Mommy into the room, followed by the unexpected appearance of my sister Doris in one of her trademark designer outfits and coordinating eyewear.

"Where's Lecia?" My grandmother entered the apartment and got out of the chair with Vincent's assistance. "She seemed a little worried on the phone and I got over here as fast as I could. Is she alright?"

"I'm sure she'll be when she sees you," I assured her.

"Doris, this is a surprise. Lecia called you too?"

"Yes Cade, and since I was in between rehearsals, I couldn't miss a family gathering, now could I?" She came over, kissed me on the cheeks and made the rounds, giving and receiving affection from all those in the room. The twins came running out of the bedroom and found their parents.

"Miles is so pretty."

"He's handsome Aria. He's a boy so we call him handsome." I attempted to correct her.

"No Uncle Cade, he's pretty. Tia Lecia has him in a long white dress with a white hat and pretty, little shoes. You'll see." Austin climbed into his father's lap. There was always a demand for Vincent's lap, a coveted spot for the three younger children. They somehow always knew who needed the lap the most and there was seldom competition for it among them.

"Austin, it's a christening gown, and you wore one when you were a baby too."

"No way. Daddy would never let me wear a dress." Vincent hugged and cuddled with his little bear cub.

"Mommy and Grammy overruled me, and all of you including your older brother Alex wore christening gowns. It's a family tradition."

"If you say so Daddy." Austin cocked his head in disbelief.

Lecia finally came out of the room smiling, with Miles cradled in her arms like he was her most precious gift, followed by Marissa, who held his pacifier and a white cotton blanket as his lady in waiting. Lecia hadn't put a lot of planning into the event, but the flowers she received from me and members of the family added to the beauty and ambiance of the space. Marisela and my mother hurried to light the candles and added the finishing touches to the table. Lecia brought Miles to Grammie Mommy, who was directing her to the center of the room to be surrounded by his family. Doris wiped a tear from her eye and went to look at Miles for the first time.

"You Moore men sure know how to make beautiful babies. Miles is gorgeous in his christening gown."

"Beautiful and he's probably talented too, just like you baby girl." Grammie Mommy never failed to give Doris her props.

"Thanks Grammie. You know I'm forever grateful to you. You gave me my first big break when I sang in your church." Grammie smiled back at her and urged us to gather around.

"We sang in her church too," Lexie reminded us.

"And what did she say Lexie, after you finished?" Doris asked, and all the children looked at each other before they chimed in with Doris.

"That was the best singing I've ever heard." Grammie had told Doris the same thing twenty years earlier.

"I should turn all of you over my knee for mocking your grandmother!" She smiled, but the children shied away in case she was serious about doing it. "Lecia, you and Cade come in front of me and let Cade take Miles into his arms while I pray." We joined hands and stood in a circle around Miles to signify the love and protection that would always surround him while he slept through the ceremony. My grandmother was long-winded in her prayers, and today was no exception. She took Miles into her arms and placed a sprinkle of water on his forehead.

She had christened so many babies in her lifetime in their homes or wherever she was summoned so we all pitched in to present her with her own christening equipment of a simple fine porcelain bowl, a matching pestle, and a container for water she prayed over before anointing the baby, all in a leather box with her initials embossed in small letters on the bottom. Aridio was the only person who remained seated as we stood around the circle.

"I've held this baby before, but I'm feeling a special prophesy as I hold him in my arms in his christening outfit. These clothes have been blessed before; I can feel it."

Aridio beamed and Marisela stepped forward and touched the hem of the garment.

"Senora Barbara, indeed the gown has been blessed. The priest in our town in the Dominican Republic held Lecia as a small baby and blessed her in this gown. The covering on his head and the shoes were worn by her twin brother, Miguel." She choked up and my mother placed an arm around her shoulder as she crossed herself. Marissa and Aridio sniffed to contain their emotions and followed Marisela in crossing themselves. Aria started squirming and kept patting her mother on the leg.

"I'm hungry Mommy. I can't stay for Grammie Mommy's properly. I'll faint if I don't get something to eat," Austin agreed.

"I'm hungry too Mommy. Can we eat now? I don't need to hear the properly either."

"It's a prophesy, Aria and Austin. Please wait until we're finished."

I had never seen Aridio or my father move so fast to address the needs of children. They almost ran into each other as my father grabbed Austin by the hand and Aridio wheeled his chair toward Aria to scoop her up and place her on his uninjured leg.

"Aridio, please be careful. I'll go with you to feed the children and I can check on the food at the same time. Will you all please excuse us?" My stomach growled again, prompting an outburst of giggles from the children. I looked out of the corner of my eye and Marissa was quietly slipping away after placing a kiss on Lecia's cheek.

"I can't stay for the *properly* either. I have rehearsals in about an hour. Gotta go." Doris drew her hands to her lips, threw kisses into the air, and grabbed her things before she hurried out the door.

"Mother, with due love and respect, I ask you to consider making the prophesy brief while I go to help Marisela with the kids." My grandmother pursed her lips and looked around the circle of family members, which was getting smaller by the minute.

"Some things can't be rushed, Lauren, and you know these things are out of my hands."

Act I. The Seed on FIre

My mother left me, Lecia, Vincent, and Dana to bear witness while she held Miles and told us of his prophecy. She closed her eyes, bowed her head, and began to speak. My parents returned to the room and stood beside me while Vincent and Dana stood next to Lecia.

"He will walk through the trials of fire, but he will not be burned. He will spend his life at the feet of his first mistress, his mystical muse, Music, a love for her he inherited from both his Tavares and Moore kindred until he meets his own muse, a young woman he'll marry and love until the end of their days." She took in a breath and seemed to tire. Lecia reached out for Miles while I went to recover Grammie's walking stick to bear her weight, but she closed her eyes again and resumed the prophecy.

"His love of music will take him on adventures throughout the world." Lecia looked at him and her mouth turned down in sadness.

"Don't worry Lecia. He won't leave us forever." I attempted to comfort her while my grandmother stared in disapproval of my interruption.

"He'll have a gift of language; however this gift will be a blessing, bringing him rewards and a curse in which he'll forever be misunderstood by others incapable of understanding his words. Miles has been blessed with the full armor of strength, and like his great-grandfather, Aaron Moore, bears the seeds of fire. As is true of his grandfather, Charles Aiden Moore, he will be able to bear smoke without damage to his lungs, and the heat of fire like his father and grandfather without damage to his limbs. He will produce the element of fire, which will cause him to withstand the consequences of its creative and destructive forces in his life."

Grammie threw her head back and sighed. She hummed softly, opened her eyes, and placed a hand on Miles's chest above his heart.

"I christen you before your family as witnesses, Miles Aridio Tavares Moore." Aridio and Marisela returned to the room with Aridio in his wheelchair and his wife who stood behind Lecia.

"Thank you, Grammie. I needed this. I needed the strength of your prayers to protect our child from all harm, hurt, and danger." Lecia thanked Grammie while a chorus of amen filled the room before all eyes turned to Miles, who was whimpering, followed by a loud wail. He began rooting at her breast, which prompted my hunger monster to growl again.

"Please enjoy the wonderful food Mami has prepared while I go feed Miles and place him down for his nap. I can't tell you what it has meant to me having you all here today. Thank you, Grammie Mommy. I'm ready for any battle coming my way, and I'll never let anyone harm my child again." We stood in silence as she left the room.

"What did she mean that he'll never be harmed again?" Marissa looked at Lecia, then at her parents.

"No more questions Marissa. Let's have a bite of food." Marisela invited us to the table.

"I know you're not sure if you and Vincent will turn Mario over to the authorities to face charges for his actions when you find him, but I'm begging you not to authorize his death. I don't want to live with his blood on my hands Cade."

"He was the one who insisted we not contact the police, and his blood won't be on your hands Lecia." I tightened my jaw and spoke through my teeth. She didn't resist me taking her into my arms as we lay in bed while Miles slept a few feet away from us in his bassinette.

"I want us to focus on raising our child instead of avenging a wrong. Mario has got to be disturbed, but he hasn't always been that way. He needs help just like Darlene needs help, and I'm sure you'll make sure she receives it."

"I hear you Lecia, and I can only promise you that Darlene will get help, but in regard to Mario, if he comes near you or Miles again or lives in the same city as you, I'll show him no mercy." She shivered in my arms.

"Are you cold?" I gathered the covers around our shoulders and settled down with her in my arms.

"I'm better now; I guess it was a chill in the air."

"Tell me about these people helping you and why you trust them more than the authorities?"

"Lecia, I can't tell you much about them because of an oath of secrecy I took, but I can tell you that I trust them with my life and the lives of my family. These men have a sworn duty to protect us, and I can't say that I trust traditional channels anymore. I'm a rich man, but I'm disillusioned that the rule of law and equal protection under the law doesn't apply to everyone in this country. There's just too much bias, and the idea of justice for all is a myth. Please let me handle this the way I feel is best for all of us. I don't want you or Miles subjected to a media frenzy."

"I don't want that either, and I may not know about these men you obviously trust, but I know and trust you."

"Thank you, Lecia, for your trust. It means a lot to me."

"Good night Cade. I love you."

"Good night Lecia. I love you and our son with all of my being."

CHAPTER THIRTEEN

Papi and Mami returned home to North Carolina after visiting with us for a week, while Marissa returned to her cousin's house to spend a few more days in New York before returning home. We were settling into a routine at the house, and I convinced Lecia, after about an hour of urging her, to go out to lunch with Dana while I stayed home with Miles.

"You need a break Lecia. We'll be alright, and I promise to call you if something happens. Don't you trust me with my own son?"

"Of course, I trust you but—"

"There's no but about it. Have fun."

The phone rang just as I had gently pushed Lecia out the door and closed it behind her.

"Cade, I need to come over and talk to you while Lecia is not there."

"Can this wait Vincent? I wanted to spend time with Miles."

"Brother, he's a newborn. He'll be asleep most of the day. I'll bet Lecia fed him before she left."

"Yes, she did. How did you know?"

"I'm the father of four. I've been around the block several times when it comes to taking care of babies."

"Alright come on over."

"I'm on my way as we speak. I'll be there shortly."

"See you then."

I checked on Miles one more time before Vincent rang the doorbell. He was quiet in his bassinette, sleeping on his back.

"So, what's so important that we couldn't talk about this tomorrow at my office?"

"Good news brother. We apprehended Mario and he fought the agents like hell so he's getting medical attention under an armed guard."

"Where was he found?" My anger vibrated in my fists.

"He was at the airport trying to board a plane to Puerto Rico and he got pulled out of the line."

"I thought he would have tried to get back to the DR where he had a better chance of avoiding discovery." I cracked my knuckles as I spoke.

"Somebody bought the ticket for him because we had surveillance on all of his accounts and there was no movement on any of them."

"He's evil, but not dumb and I'm relieved he was caught. As soon as Lecia returns, you can take me to him, so I can extract my revenge." I smiled thinking of all the things I planned to do to him.

"Not so quick little brother. It seems that Mr. Rodriguez has some shady friends whom are of interest to The Network. They need to talk to him first before you get to settle the score. In the meantime, I have the psychiatrist's report on Darlene Evans."

"Oh…that. Have a seat so we can go over it. Any surprises?"

"Not really. The assessment and report were completed by two independent psychiatrists, and they concluded without doubt she was mentally ill at the time of the attack on Lecia. They felt Mario manipulated her by taking advantage of her psychotic obsession with you and he masterminded the entire scheme. The only thing Mario and Darlene agreed upon was to spare Lecia's life. They both wanted to take Miles away from her, but even in her psychotic state, Darlene didn't want to kill Lecia. Both psychiatrists reported Darlene still saw Lecia as a friend but felt even her friends had to pay for their mistakes, especially one as grave as taking you away from her. Lecia tricked you into marrying her, according to Darlene."

"What the hell? I never loved Darlene, and nothing could be further from the truth."

"I know but I need to be sure you're alright with the money you transferred into Darlene's account being used for her treatment."

"Yes, it's better than my initial intent to use it for her execution. If she wasn't found to be mentally ill, I would have made sure she rotted in hell."

"So, tell me how the agents in the Network convinced her to confess?"

"We're in New York, and there's always a film set available that looks like a police department. We hired extras to play the roles of employees at the station. It didn't hurt that she was given a sedative to cloud her consciousness. We employed the usual good cop/bad cop routine to turn her against him. She thought Mario had snitched on her, so she began snitching on him, which led us to Miles and then to Mario."

"Lecia has been asking questions about the Network."

"I suggest you keep your answers as vague as possible. The less she knows, the better at this point. If something happens and this gets out in the press, she can plead plausible deniability of all the facts, while you, on the other hand, can lie with credibility."

"I had a good teacher, brother."

"I'm glad I did my job well." He turned his head in the direction of the sound coming from the nursery. "Is that my nephew?"

"Yes, I have the baby monitor on. He can't be hungry. Lecia fed him before she left, but I'll go heat up a bottle just in case."

"Alex was the same way. It's as if he had a sixth sense and knew when his mother wasn't at home. Let me go get him while you warm up a bottle. I need some bonding time with my nephew."

"Thanks, I'll be right back."

It didn't take long to warm up a bottle, but by the time I got back to the living area, Lecia was back home kissing Miles on the forehead while he squirmed in his uncle's arms. I handed the bottle to Vincent, who fed Miles just before the fussing began.

"What happened? I thought you were going to have lunch with the girls." Her attention wavered between me and Vincent holding our son.

"I wasn't hungry, and I couldn't stop worrying—I mean, thinking about Miles. Why is he awake? He shouldn't be hungry. Has he been fretful the entire time I've been gone?" She looked on as he seized the bottle's nipple, hungry for nurturance.

"He just started whimpering so I got him a bottle." I remained strong under the interrogation as Miles turned his head and the nipple slipped out of his mouth. Vincent tried to reposition himself and the bottle in his mouth, but Miles turned his head again and began wailing.

"Vincent, I'll take him." Lecia took him from Vincent.

"Sometimes a baby just wants his mother, but it doesn't mean you have to be here every time he's a little anxious. His father was here and so was I." Vincent gave her the baby.

"I know, and I don't doubt Cade's ability to take care of him or how good you both are with your children. It's not that, it's just my own anxieties. I was too uncomfortable to enjoy time away from him. I'm not ready yet, but I get your point." She cuddled him, and he settled back to a quiet slumber.

"Did you miss Mommy?" Lecia kissed Miles on the cheeks.

"Mommy sure missed you. I'll take him back to the nursery. Vincent, it was good seeing you again, and tell Dana I'll call her. I love spending time with her, but she knows what it's like having a new baby."

"I'm sure she understands." He took his phone out of his pocket and looked at the message.

"Lecia, do you mind if Cade walks downstairs with me. I need to leave but I also need to share something with him."

"Sure, Miles and I will be fine until he gets back. Cade, I love you and I appreciate how thoughtful you were giving me a break. A little sunshine and a ride around the corner were all I needed. If you need to go out with Vincent, we'll be here when you get back." She leaned over to kiss me before taking Miles back to his room.

"This shouldn't take too long Cade. I need your help with something." I didn't know what my brother had planned, but I grabbed my wallet and keys to follow him out of the apartment.

We exited the front door and emerged into blinding sunlight shining down on a warm spring day. It seemed ironic how many sunny days we were having the past week in contrast to the week before when I had to depend on all the inner strength I had to survive the darkest period of my life. I put on my shades and followed Vincent, who was motioning me to follow to him to a dark limousine waiting at the curb. The back window descended, and even though Vincent prepared me in the elevator to expect to see Darlene in the car, I recoiled at the sight of her seated and struggling against the weight of two men seated beside her. I made haste to get in the vehicle to stop her from drawing the attention of people enjoying a leisurely walk before they got closer to the car. I entered the car and sat facing her while Vincent got in the front seat near the driver.

"Cade, I knew you would come back to me." She tried reaching for me but was restrained.

"I got the money you sent, and we'll have enough to get away from here together. Go get our son and we can be a family." Her lids were getting heavier as she spoke. Her two attendants repositioned her comfortably in the seat as she slid down and slumped forward.

"What happens from here Vincent?" I turned to face my brother.

"I can address that, sir. I'm one of her attendants, and she was given a very mild sedative just in case she became agitated while talking to you. She became less agitated just knowing she would see you again before we take her to the facility for treatment."

"I see. Darlene?"

"Yes, Cade my darlin," she responded in her drug-induced haze.

"I've come to tell you goodbye. I hope you get the treatment you need, and I've been assured that some of the best doctors and effective treatments are available at this facility."

"Cade, please don't leave me. I don't need treatment. I love you and all I need is you."

I said nothing more and placed my hand on the latch to open the door. Vincent followed behind me, and after closing the door, I hit the roof of the car with a firm slap to signal the driver to leave. I turned my back on the car pulling off from the curb, on Darlene, and on any memories associated with her. I could only hope, with time, Lecia and I would be able to process this unfortunate experience and move on with our lives.

The limo was out of view by the time I turned to look back and focus on the scenery before me, as if seeing it for the first time. The tree-lined streets, bright flowers swaying in the breeze in large stone urns, and the warmth of the sun on my face comforted me. Vincent placed his hand on my arm to gain my attention.

"One more thing Cade. What do you want to have happen to Mario if The Network has their own plans and they don't want you involved in it?"

"I don't give a damn what happens to Mario, but I would like the opportunity to face him."

"Alright, but he may be taken care of without involving you, and we won't have to discuss this ever again. If questioned about his whereabouts, you can't admit to what you don't know."

I headed back to the apartment and quickened my pace to return to Lecia as a wave of anger descended upon me. I felt nothing but rage toward Mario for the hell he'd put my family through. He had no right to decide my son's birthday.

His birthday was supposed to be April 28th, three days before the twins' birthday on May 1st. Vincent caught up with me and, through my blind fury, I pulled away from him and clenched my teeth in anger.

"Lecia doesn't need to see you like this. I'm begging you to calm down."

I pressed the button for the elevator and grew more impatient with the wait. I was relieved the car was empty, and I took a deep breath as I stepped in, with the knowledge that my brother had always been in my corner and I knew he was right. I needed to get a handle on myself, and it was my mother's comforting voice in my head that provided me the ability to calm down. *It doesn't matter at this point when he was born. We must be grateful that he survived the experience and we have our baby back where he belongs and where he is safe.*

"I'm alright." I took another deep breath and assured Vincent before the elevator door opened. We returned to the apartment and found Lecia talking on the phone as we entered the living room.

"Cade, I'm glad you're back. Dr. Roberts is on the phone. He had some information he wanted to share with us." I hurried to the couch and took a seat near her.

"Dr. Roberts, do you mind if I place you on speaker, so you can talk with both of us and my brother-in-law, Vincent Moore?"

"Sure. I wanted to share some things with you before your checkup."

"You're on speaker now," Lecia informed him as Vincent and I acknowledged our presence.

"The pathologist had a chance to examine your placenta we sent to him, and I'm so glad Vincent and Cade had the presence of mind to gather all the evidence on the night you were assaulted and wrap it up after they discovered it near you. It looked like your placenta had separated spontaneously from your uterine wall, and the pathologist confirmed my suspicions that you experienced a condition that I'm sure you're aware of, a placental abruption." I leaned toward the phone Lecia had placed on the table to talk to the doctor.

"This is Cade. What is that doctor?"

"Hello Cade. It's a very serious condition that could have resulted in Lecia's death and the death of your son if it hadn't been caught as soon as it was detected. Your baby's abductor, in a twisted case of fate, was a good Samaritan. If he or she and any accomplices hadn't delivered the baby, Lecia may have bled to death. Her contractions weren't all from the meds but also from her body trying to expel the placenta. This was a medical emergency. Do you all know anything about the people involved in this?"

"Dr. Roberts, this is Vincent Moore. I appreciate your willingness to step into this case after you were contacted by some long-term associates of mine, and we're grateful for your discretion in this matter. The abduction is still under investigation."

"You're welcome, but you know I have much respect for Lecia's original obstetrician, Dr. Young, and I don't want to ruin my professional relationship with him."

"I assure you Cade and I have addressed this with him regarding the transfer of care since there was an initial concern that someone in his office could have been an accomplice to this crime, but we're in the process of ruling that out."

"Lecia are you comfortable with the plan to have me see you at your six weeks checkup?"

"Yes, I signed the release to have my records transferred to your practice, and I would appreciate it if you would continue to follow me."

"Alright, I'll see you at your scheduled follow up. Good bye Lecia."

"Goodbye Dr. Roberts." Lecia ended the call and remained quiet for a moment.

"It's going to take some time to wrap my head around this. So, I'm supposed to thank Darlene for what she's done to me?" she asked me, and I took her into my arms.

"You don't owe Darlene anything, and you should take as much time as you need to sort out your feelings. It's confusing for me, and I'm sure it's as confusing as hell for you."

"It is." She choked back her emotions and leaned into my chest for comfort.

"Well, I guess I should be going. I promised Dana I'd be home to help her with the kids, so she could prepare some new recipes she's been dying to try." Lecia leaned up to address him.

"Thanks Vincent."

"Lecia, let me walk Vincent to the door and I'll be right back." I kissed her forehead and led Vincent to the door.

"Thanks, brother, for everything."

"You bet, but you know I'll always have your back. Call you later."

"Bye." I closed the door behind him and returned to the couch to take Lecia in my arms.

"We're safe and we'll be okay. We have the support and prayers of a lot of people who love us."

CHAPTER FOURTEEN

Miles-Three weeks old

We were exhausted, and I didn't need to look at a clock any longer. Miles had taken over as the official timekeeper: 3 a.m., 6 a.m., 9 a.m., noon, 3 p.m., 6 p.m., 9 p.m., midnight, repeat.

I took off time from the club to help Lecia, as she adamantly refused to have someone come into the house to help us. All her energies had been focused on the baby, and she agreed to pump her milk, so I could help with the early morning and late-night feedings. This had been our schedule for almost a month and my parents were due to arrive any moment to enter our cocoon. The apartment was a mess, we looked a mess in clean but wrinkled clothing, and I didn't care. Our little Aria was a great helper and came to our home often, even when her siblings stopped coming over after Miles baptized each of them with regurgitated breast milk.

"I'll get it," I yelled out to Lecia and went to answer the door. My parents, followed by Vincent and Dana, walked in.

"Hello Cade, we've come to stage an intervention." My mother hugged me and entered the room. She stopped in her tracks and surveyed the clothes and assorted baby things scattered around the room. Lecia came in and hugged everyone.

"Sorry about how things look. Just push it aside and have a seat."

"Both of you look like the walking dead. The baby isn't sleeping more than three hours at a time yet?"

"No, and he was fretful last night. Some babies take a little longer to sleep more than four hours at a time Lauren. Cade has been a real trooper throughout this, and we're making it."

"That's why we're here. You haven't let anyone help you other than the one- or two-hours Aria comes to visit, and I'm not sure how helpful a four-year-old child is."

"Lecia, you really look tired, and I know you promised my girl she could help, but is she adding to your list of things to do?" Dana asked.

"No, she really is great with Miles. You and Vincent would be so proud if you saw how often he stopped crying and just looked at her while I changed his diaper and gave him a bath. The two of them have bonded so well with each other." Charles Aiden cleared his throat and added to the discussion.

"I understand that the two of you have been traumatized by the situation surrounding Miles' birth but staying here in this protective cocoon and not letting others help you isn't the answer."

My parents had started referring to the abduction as "the situation." Only recently had my mother been able to talk about it without choking up.

"Charles Aiden, we appreciate your concern and those of everyone here, but Miles still gets fretful in the evening and when I'm not immediately available because I'm taking a nap." My mother went to Lecia and placed her hand on her shoulder.

"Lecia and Cade, we're not here to tell you how to raise your child or talk about the consequences of hovering too much over him. You're a nurse practitioner, and you know this already. Just let us help you." I stood up and tried to take some of the pressure off Lecia.

"Miles was snatched out of his mother's womb. You don't think that was traumatic for him and that we should do all we can to comfort him when he needs it? I don't mean to be so graphic, but this has been difficult for us." I looked at Vincent for support.

"Brother, do you think Miles becomes fretful because he's sensing his parents' anxiety?"

"It's possible. I can't say I haven't noticed that he's calmer when I'm calm and singing to him."

My father piped in again, as I was less defensive in my response. "Son, none of us want to model fear for Miles. You're not a fearful person, and I've always admired how slow to anger you were before this happened. You don't want him afraid of his own shadow, do you?"

"You know I love you like a sister Lecia, and you've helped us raise our four children," Dana added. "I've learned the hard way that it's not good to respond to every whimper they make. He needs time and space to develop his own way to self-soothe." Lecia and I both turned to the sound of our son's soft purrs over the baby monitor.

"He sounds okay," my mother reminded us. "How will he ever learn to soothe himself if you respond to his every sound? Give him a chance to develop that skill. He deserves it and, more importantly, you'll start practicing it today. Your father and I will spend the night here and Vincent and Dana will help clean the apartment. The baby monitor will be moved out of your bedroom so that the two of you can get at least eight hours of sleep or even twelve hours if you like." We both gave my mother, Lauren Vivienne Moore, blank stares as she looked back at us with her hands on her hips.

"What are you waiting for? I'll see you both later. Miles will be fine."

We were both too tired to argue, so I took Lecia by the hand, walked to the bedroom, and crawled into bed. I was asleep before my head hit the pillow.

⁓

"What? I got it. I got…." I shook the fog out of my head and looked at the clock. It was 1:30 am, and I grabbed my phone to answer it before Lecia heard it buzzing.

"This is Vincent."

"Yeah, I know that. I thought you wanted me to get some sleep." I kept my voice as low as possible to avoid waking Lecia and leaned over the side of the bed.

"Sorry Cade to tell you this, but Mario escaped custody during the transfer from one facility to another."

"What the hell?"

"My question exactly—but don't worry, we'll find him."

"If you don't, I will, and he's a dead man." I ended the call.

Lecia was starting to stir, and I got back under the covers.

"What's wrong Cade?"

"Ah…just the sound system malfunctioned at the club, but it's under control."

"Do you have to go in to handle it?"

"No, they just wanted to let me know what was happening. Let's get some more rest."

She settled on my chest and closed her eyes while I rubbed her back to coax her back to sleep.

CHAPTER FIFTEEN

Miles-Six weeks old

We had gotten a little more rest this past week as Lecia had become comfortable letting Miles stay with Vincent, Dana, and the kids for a few hours while we took care of last-minute errands. The time finally arrived for us to board the plane to take Miles on his first trip to North Carolina, where he was sure to be a much sought after little boy. He slept through most of the flight but was awake and squirming by the time we walked through the front door of my parents' home. Lecia's father had been under the weather, so he and her mother hadn't made the trip back up to New York since his birth. They had called several times yesterday to make sure we didn't intend to spend most of this visit with my family and deprive his maternal relatives of their time with the newest member of the family. I was still on paternity leave, and a get together with my band members, many of whom hailed from the Carolinas, was also on the list of things to do on an already packed schedule. Lecia knew a gynecologist in Charlotte and she cancelled her appointment back home in New York. We would be in town awhile and we had the benefit of many babysitters.

I looked over at my son, busy sucking his fists and starting to whimper.

"I think he wants to feed," Lecia confirmed my suspicions as she kissed his forehead while I struggled to get in the door with my arms filled with baby stuff. "Just a little longer, my angel."

We had been in the foyer for seconds before my mother took Miles out of Lecia's arms and began cradling him and cooing grandmother affections.

"I'm so glad you got home safely, and I can't tell you how happy we are to finally have the baby here." Other family members encircled her and Miles while pushing me and Lecia to the side. My father took him, followed by my grandmother and a host of uncles and cousins, lavishing affection on him.

"Thanks, it's good to be here." I half-jokingly made the announcement on mine and Lecia's behalf, as we were clearly not the ones the family members were waiting to see anymore.

"Oh, Cade, of course we were looking forward to seeing you and Lecia, but having the baby here is going to be such a treat." At that point Miles wailed in protest of his stomach not being filled on demand. I put down my baby stuff, pushed through the crowd, and took him out of my grandmother's hands after she had worked so hard to get a hold of him again.

"Grammie, let me take him off your hands. He's getting a little testy because he's hungry. We'll be right back." I scooped him up, ruffling her feathers, and whisked him and Lecia to our bedroom.

"Stay here and feed him while I try to smooth things over. I knew Miles was going to be the star of this show, but I wasn't expecting it as soon as we got here. If you didn't know how possessive my family is with their babies, you're about to find out. Things get a little crazy when a newborn is in the house. Everyone looks at him like a new-found treasure."

"Interesting, but he's a Tavares too Cade."

"I know Lecia. I'm just speaking from experience." Lecia sat on the bed rocking him and trying to settle him down to nurse him.

"I think he was hungry and a little overstimulated. I'll put him down for his nap before I come join you. Good luck." I leaned over and gave them both a kiss on the forehead.

"Thanks, and I'll be needing it." I closed the door behind me and girded my loins for the battle. The family had gathered in the kitchen by the time I returned, and I faced the stern faces of my parents and grandmother. Vincent and Dana had come over, and I sighed in relief that I had some reinforcements.

"Hi Vincent and Dana. When did you all get here?"

"We flew in last night and decided to come over—and from the looks of things, not a moment too soon. Let me guess, you ended the welcome home Miles party too soon?"

"Yeah, I guess it was something like that." By the look of things, as I surveyed the faces in the room, I was found guilty of the crime. My grandmother opened her mouth, which I assumed was to speak the verdict and deliver my sentence while I remained calm and silent. I hoped the narrative would shift by the presence of her royal cuteness herself, my niece Aria, who had come skipping into the kitchen.

"Hello, Uncle Cade," she came toward me and gave me a kiss on the cheek. I scooped her up, giving her affection and providing myself with a little protection from the irritation of our relatives.

"Hello my darling Aria. It's good to see you again." She cocked her head and raised an eyebrow.

"Uncle Cade, you're being funny. You just saw me two days ago." She chuckled and resumed talking, oblivious to the tension in the room. "I just came out of the room with Tia Lecia and Miles and I've never seen him nurse so fast and for so long. Didn't you feed him on the plane?"

"No, he surprised us by sleeping throughout the flight, and I guess he's hungry now." The atmosphere was starting to shift in my favor, thanks to the testimony of my expert witness and ally, Aria. *I love this kid!*

My grandmother was the first to break the silence of the adults who had taken a seat at the table and Aria's observations relaxed the scowls on their faces. "So how was the flight with the baby, Kaiden?" My eyes met Vincent's, knowing it wasn't a good sign Barbara was referring to me by my given name. I guided Aria to a seat at the table near me.

"Miles was calm and slept through most of it. The little bit of turbulence didn't bother him too much."

"That's good," my mother added. "It shouldn't be a problem then for us to come get him to spend time with us here, especially this winter when it's cold up there."

"Mom, I'm sure you understand that I'll need to talk to Lecia about it since the baby's not even six months old yet."

"He's never too young to get to know his family. So far, he's only spent time with your brother and his family. We're glad you and your brother are so close, but our family is much larger than that Kaiden." I looked at Vincent and Dana, who were looking up and away from me.

So much for help from my reinforcement. My father, who so far had been keeping his thoughts to himself, now entered his motion.

"We understand Miles is your first child and you and Lecia want to give him your full attention, but we love him too and we hope you won't be selfish with him. He needs time to get to know us too, and the sooner the better," and with that, the tension started to mount again. Aria turned her head and pointed to the door, where Lecia was coming in with Miles. She had freshened him up and changed his clothes. She smiled and placed him in my mother's arms.

"Hello everyone, we're back." I sighed and hoped all was right in my world again. Miles was back in the circle of love again, as all the adults got up from the table to look down on him. He managed to open his eyes to the delight of our adoring relatives. Lecia beamed with the pride of a new mother, and my parents looked at the baby and then at me.

"You did good son. He's a beautiful boy," my father remarked, and I puffed up my chest as I looked at my son stretching and yawning before his lids descended over his eyes. *Thanks babe,* I mouthed to Lecia, grateful for the reprieve. I knew my parents were right that we had to share more of our time with them now that we had a child.

"I'm going to play with Lexie, Uncle Cade." I took it as Aria's cue to help her out of the chair. She placed a kiss on Miles' forehead, whom my grandmother had taken from my mother.

"Come on, Grammie Mommy. Lexie wanted to show you her new dance move. She's been practicing it for her recital. Let's go find her." I got up to take Miles from her.

"I'll be right back." She relinquished her hold on him and got up to go with Aria to find Lexie. I sat back in my chair and held his body close to my nose, inhaling a whiff of sweet baby scent. Miles yawned and opened his eyes. I smiled at him as he cooed at me; his sounds were music to my ears. I bent to kiss him on the cheeks and his breath smelled of warm sugar cookies. I was intoxicated with the vision of my child, which was even more unbelievable, taking in the fact that I once questioned if I wanted children, and now I couldn't get enough of the miracle of having him in our lives. I got up again and placed him in my father's arms. I was aware with all the attention he had gotten from the female relatives that my father may have felt left out.

I observed my father looking down at Miles with misty eyes and attempting to swallow a hard lump in his throat. He wanted to say something, but the words seemed stuck somewhere between his heart and vocal chords. There was a quiet simplicity to the moment of brown eyes looking at young hazel eyes, but it also felt deeper and more profound.

"He reminds me of you, Kaiden." The lump in his throat must have been contagious as I absorbed the emotions ignited by my father's comment. My mother, Lecia, and Dana sat looking at them, and Vincent pulled out his phone and motioned for me to go closer to my father.

"Let me take a picture of three generations of Moore men." I got up and stood behind my father while Vincent took the picture, capturing the first image of multi-generational male bonding between me, my father, and my son. I looked back and a picture of my grandfather, Aaron Moore, was in the background. Lecia had gone back to our room and gotten her camera so we could capture more shots of Miles' first homecoming to my childhood home. It surprised us that he stayed awake for most of the picture-taking session and even delivered his first social smile to the delight of all in the room. Not long afterwards, a strong smell alerted us it was time for a diaper change. Lecia took him and disappeared from the room.

"Vincent, go get the boys, and Cade, can you get Miles and join us in my study?" My father rose from his chair to head to his study.

"Sure, I'll meet you there." I was glad Lecia was out of earshot since she had problems with my father's male bonding room even though she was aware his study wasn't off limits to the female members of the family.

"I want to welcome Miles into the Moore men club on his first visit to North Carolina."

Dana had married into the family almost ten years ago and wasn't offended by my father's Moore men meetings; Lecia on the other hand was still getting used to the idea. I sat at the table after my father and Vincent left, wondering how I was going to present it to her. She had concerns about exposing Miles to anything that promoted paternalistic ideas in the family, and I wasn't sure if she would be cool about this even though he was only six weeks old. She returned to the kitchen without Miles. Dana spoke to her as she was entering the room.

"Lexie and Aria have a guest visiting with them. Their friend Briana is here so you and I can have some tea while Cade takes care of Miles." Dana got up and began placing items on the table to share a cup of tea and conversation together with Lecia and my mother just as Aria was returning to the room to speak with her mother.

"Dana, I just put Miles down for his nap. It's been a long day for him since we had to get up so early. He should be alright in his bassinette." She looked at me and smiled.

"Mommy, Lexie is playing with Briana, and Grammie Mommy said she was tired and was going to take a nap. I'm going to the study with Daddy and my brothers, alright?"

"Sure Aria."

"Let's go get Miles, Uncle Cade." She began pulling me from the room as if no permission to attend the male gathering was required and her desire to be with us wasn't going to be denied.

"But—" Lecia started to speak up but shrugged and decided against it.

"Don't worry Tia Lecia, I'll make sure Miles is alright." She waved at Lecia, then took my hand and walked out with her head held high and confident. Her father and I had always told her she had the same rights and privileges as her male relatives—something we had instilled in her and her sister since their births. We went to the bedroom and gathered my sleeping son before heading to my father's study, where he was waiting to give me and Vincent expensive imported cigars.

I took a seat and looked at my father sitting behind his desk while Alex stood beside him, scribbling on a sheet of paper, and Austin sat in Vincent's lap. I cradled Miles in my arms as he slept, sweet and placid. He didn't stir despite Aria kissing him on his forehead and swinging his little hand up and down. Warm feelings descended upon me, and I relaxed as I looked at my son with pride. One year ago, I sat in this same room with my father surrounded by me, Vincent, and his sons. My father had taken great pride in all his children, but I knew the ritual of the gathering of the males of the clan in his study was important to him, although it had changed over the years.

When Vincent and I both turned twenty-one, we were offered cigars to smoke with our father, and as the kids started coming along, the ritual of inviting the children in for bonding time with Grandpa began. Lexie was like my sister Doris in that she never cared to stay around us males talking about sports and fishing—but Aria, she came most of the time there was a gathering.

Act I. The Seed on FIre

"This is a very important day for me as the head of this family, although secretly, I know your mother would beg to differ who's actually the head of the family, but for this day and in this room, I stake my claim to the title." We smiled with my father as we had all heard it before.

"Cade, my son, this is the first time you present your son to our gathering. I pray that my third grandson, Miles Aridio Moore, may know a life of health, happiness, and prosperity." We raised our glasses, some filled with fine liquor, and others with apple juice.

"Here, here," a congratulatory chorus filled the room and I felt on top of the world. My lungs expanded to their fullest and I took in deep, satisfied breaths, inhaling pride and support from other members of my family and exhaling relief that I had my son back and he was safe with his family.

"Look at this, guys." Alex, Austin and Aria looked to their father, whose big personality always got the attention of those around him.

"Say something to Miles and watch what happens. He's been asleep since his dad brought him in the room despite Aria's attempts to wake him up."

"Miles." They took turns calling out his name and he stayed asleep. Vincent gave Aria a sideways glance, often knowing her intentions, especially when she was being mischievous. I continued cradling him in my arms and cocked one eyebrow. *Where's he going with this.*

"Say something Uncle Cade." Aria bounced up and down, eager to see what was about to happen but unable to wait for it.

"Miles, wake up baby." She stroked his cheek and kissed him, and he drew his eyelids even tighter before relaxing them in sleep. I lifted him to face me, cradling his head and buttocks safely in my hands.

"Miles, it's Daddy. Hey, my son, it's your daddy." He began squirming in my hands and struggling to open his eyes as I moved him away from the light shining on him from a lamp nearby. He opened his sweet little mouth and yawned before blinking open his eyes.

Vincent laughed, and the other children opened their mouths in surprise as if the most profound event had just occurred.

"I noticed last week that every time he heard his parents' voice, no matter how sleepy he was, he would open his eyes and selectively track their voices. I believe he already knows who his parents are. Keep talking to him Cade."

"Is that true buddy? You already know who your daddy is? Do you know how much I love you?" He stared at me, his eyes soft and filled with an inner glow that belied his age, locked on mine with laser focus. I kissed his forehead and my heart felt full of gratitude. I loved his mother with all my heart but my boy, my *Mile-sy*, had his own share of my heart carved out.

"We love him too Uncle Cade," Aria piped in. "His eyes were green like mine, but they seem to be turning brown. I wanted him to keep his green eyes." She frowned and crossed her arms, but Miles kept staring at me, unfazed by Aria's physical contact with him. "He won't stop looking at you Uncle Cade. I wonder what he's thinking."

"He's thinking maybe that he feels the love in this room and he wants to get to know all of us better." I knew I was projecting my hopes and dreams of having a close and meaningful relationship with him.

"Cade let me hold him and you'll see how fast he falls back asleep." Vincent placed Austin on the couch and got up so that I could hand Miles to him, who was turning his head in my direction as he was carried away by his uncle.

"He's longing to be with you; look at him still looking back at you." He fretted briefly, and Vincent held him close to his chest, then held him away from his body to allow us to see his eyelids descending and his body going limp with sleep.

"Let me hold him Vincent." My father always preferred holding a sleeping baby instead of one who was awake. Miles slept in my father's arms while Aria and Austin gravitated to their father and sat in his lap.

"Stop tickling us Daddy," they both squealed with delight. My father took Miles' fingers into his and looked up at me.

"So how are things going Cade?" My father asked.

"Members of the band are coming to Charlotte this weekend. You know Mike and Wolf still own homes here and regularly commute between Charlotte and New York. We plan to discuss the possibility of accepting a contract for a world tour sometime this year."

I thought I should at least start sharing my ideas about the possibility of touring with my family. I didn't think it would come as a surprise to them since I had been in the entertainment industry for years. I saw Vincent shaking his head out of the corner of my eyes as I answered my father's question. Aria got up out of her father's lap and went to hug Miles.

"Well, I can't say I was expecting you to consider a new contract so soon."

"We have some hot tracks and you have to tour when your music's hot." Vincent cleared his throat.

"Does that mean you'll be gone for another year Uncle Cade?" Alex looked up from his pad he had been scribbling notes on.

"Maybe, but I won't be alone. I'm planning on taking Lecia and Miles with me." Vincent started choking and his eyes widened.

"Nooo!" Aria screeched like a wounded animal and ran out of the room.

"Oh, oh. That can't be good. I think I left something in my room." Alex gathered his pad and left.

"Yeah, something in his room." Austin jumped out of his father's lap and scurried out the room.

"I tried to warn you, Kaiden." Vincent frowned at me. "You still don't read cues well do you?"

"What cues Vincent? I'm not as in tune to your children as you are. Are you assuming I should be?"

"I tried warning you that Aria was listening, and didn't you see how she looked at Miles? She's upset that you may be leaving us and taking your family with you. You've got to know how much she's bonded to all of you."

"I do know that, and I'm sorry if I wasn't sensitive to her feelings." I ran my hand through my hair and let out a deep sigh.

"She has probably run to her mother for comfort, and Dana will tell our mother who will tell Lecia and they should all be heading for us in four, three, two, one."

Lecia came in first and looked around the room until she spotted Miles in my father's lap.

"I'll take Miles from you, Charles Aiden." She took him into her arms and he opened his eyes, startled by the movement, but settled back down as she rubbed his back.

"Rest my sweet baby while I speak to your daddy." He snuggled, into the planes of her chest and closed his eyes, returning to peaceful slumber.

I didn't think peace was something Daddy was going to get.

"Cade, don't you think you could have discussed a matter as important as a world tour and separation from the family for one year with me first, before you upset that child?" My shoulders dropped, and I rubbed my chest in imagined pain.

"I was just thinking out loud and nothing has been settled. Of course, I planned to discuss it with you because I couldn't agree to the tour if you and Miles weren't with me."

Dana and my mother entered the room and flanked Lecia on both sides while Aria initially stayed behind them but eventually stepped forward and pulled at the hem of my mother's dress.

"Do something Grammie. I don't want to lose Miles." She hid her face in my mother's dress.

My mother patted her head and looked at me with the all too familiar drawn eyebrows and pursed lips.

This matter is far from being settled. If I got this much resistance from my family, I could only imagine what tomorrow would be like if I broached the subject of leaving with Lecia's family.

The house was quiet early in the wee hours of this morning, and Lecia was in bed asleep when I got up to go to the kitchen to get some water. After dinner, my mother had retired to her study and I hadn't seen her for the remainder of the evening. That was something she did occasionally. When we were younger, she would announce to my father and us three kids that she needed some time for herself, especially when my father chose to spend long days and nights at the office instead of coming home or one of us kids declared an unrelenting war of whining and complaining about the other. As the youngest member of the family, I was the one who would eventually go in her room and coax her to join the family. There was not much expected of me as my mother's baby except being the one elected to let my mother know how much we loved and needed her. I was the one always given the responsibility of being the contrite one, which wasn't bad because it came with perks.

My father would seek me out to have me talk to her and reward me for my services. If Vincent or Doris needed my services because they had upset Mom, as teenagers are known to do, I somehow got a pardon to do whatever I wanted to do and they either took the blame or sided with me when I needed allies in the negotiations with my parents. Tonight, I was the one who had made Mom sad, and I didn't like it. My attention turned to the sounds of voices, probably the television, coming from the family room. I placed my glass in the sink and followed the sounds. A faint blue light escaped into the hall and lighted my way to the scene of my mother dabbing the corner of her eye while she leaned over what appeared to be old photo albums.

"Mom, everything alright?" She placed the balled-up piece of tissue in the pocket of her robe.

"Yes, everything is fine. What are you doing up this time of morning?" I came toward her and sat in the chair facing her.

"I needed a glass of water and heard sounds coming from the room. When did you become a night owl?" Small talk was always something that proceeded a deeper discussion between us, and I was grateful she was willing to engage in it with me.

"Sometimes I don't sleep well. I guess it's something that comes with aging, and often I'll pull out pictures of you all as kids because it relaxes me to remember a simpler time."

"Was it really simpler when you had three small kids and all their friends running around the house?" A smile spread across her face and I leaned forward to view pictures of the three of us in the backyard. Vincent and I were dripping wet in our swimsuits and Doris, seated in a lounger with her hair pulled back in a ponytail and oversized white rimmed glasses covering her eyes, was looking like the star she thought she had become.

"Cade, in some ways it was simpler because I felt I knew you all much better than I do today. Vincent was always the take charge one as the oldest, and I knew someday he would go out into the world to stake his claim just as your father had done. Doris, bless her heart, was my only girl and Lord knows I love her, but she came here a diva and will leave this world a diva. She's been told all her life how pretty she is and the fact that she can sing like a songbird clinched her fate. I knew she wanted to be out in the world and she belonged to the world. Our home would just be a place of respite for her—but you Cade, I knew you were the last child whom I would bring into this world. Do you remember what you always told me even as a little boy?"

"I told you a lot of things, but I'm not sure what was most memorable, so tell me." I sat back in my chair.

"You told me when you grew up, you would meet a woman just like me and you would marry her. Do you remember that?"

"Vaguely," I gazed inward, trying to recall the conversation, then looked at her, seeing the mist of tears covering her eyes again.

"Well, what I allowed myself over time to believe was the second part of your promise. You told me you'd come back to me and you would bring wonderful babies with you for me to love because you knew how much I loved my babies. I always knew Vincent and Doris would leave, but you Cade, I thought I would have you and all the babies. I'm just a little sad that you plan to leave with your first baby and he won't have a chance to get to know me."

My chest heaved as if struggling against an emotional weight. She may have not intended to do it, but she'd dropped an emotional load on me. I had disappointed my mother and I needed to fix it. After all, that was my job in the Moore family. I went to the couch and took her into my arms, but she spoke before I had a chance to say anything further.

"You don't have to fix this or make things right for me Cade. I realize you've tried to do that all your life and I need to let you know that while I may not agree with your decision, I know I'll have to accept it. You're a man now and not some little boy with a big heart. I'm proud of you and you have to do what's right for your family."

"Mom, you've always had a good read on me, and I think that's what made it easy for me to connect with you in a way I thought I couldn't connect with other members of the family. I was never just little Cade who didn't have a right to my own thoughts and feelings in this family with you. Some days it was damn hard being the youngest in a family full of stars."

"You always had your own light Cade, and you have a right to let it shine. No one, including me, has the right to hold you back from your destiny. I want all of you to be all you can be, even if it means I'll miss you. We can make this work and I'm a little sad because I don't know how to do that just yet."

"Can we agree to sleep on it and see how we feel about it later? Lecia and I haven't discussed it yet so it's still up in the air." I gave her one final hug before helping her to her feet and ushering her back to bed.

"I love you Cade."

"I love you Mom, and I can't tell you how much it has meant to me to bring my son home to you."

"No words are needed. I see it in your eyes." I led her into the hall and went back to grab a little more sleep before our trip to the Tavares' celebration for Miles later today.

Michele Sims

CHAPTER SIXTEEN

Traveling with Miles wasn't cumbersome because he was a fretful baby—to the contrary, he was usually not fussy and loved the steady movement of the car. It was Lecia who insisted that we carry his stroller, mobile bassinette, baby bag filled with clothing and personal effects, bottles of milk, and her breast pump.

"Do you really think all this is necessary for a day trip across town? I'm sure your parents have supplies for him, including a bassinette," I grumbled as I gathered some of his things while the limo driver grabbed the rest. We were accompanied by security guards, but I instructed them to stay within a discrete distance so that they wouldn't discourage Mario from coming out of the shadows. I was almost certain his family—not Marco but his mother—had something to do with his ability to evade capture for the last three weeks.

"Yes Cade, all this is necessary, and you didn't have to come if this was a burden to you to visit with my family." I got a grip on the bags and headed up the walk with her.

"I trust you to keep our son safe, but your safety is in my hands since you're at risk of running into Mario, so of course, I was going to accompany you. End of story Lecia." We arrived at the door and I struggled to free one of my fingers to ring the doorbell.

"It's probably not locked, just push the door." I noticed the door wasn't completely closed and pushed it with my foot.

"Your parents don't lock their doors and you want to be here with Miles?"

She entered the foyer and stopped to face me while rocking Miles, dressed in a light blue cotton outfit with matching blue socks and white shoes and wrapped in the lightweight blanket his abuela had crocheted for him.

"Listen Cade, I don't want you scrutinizing everything my family does while we're here. This is Miles' first visit to my family's home, and I want the visit to be a pleasant one, alright?"

"Sure Lecia. I'll be on my best behavior, but I still don't think it's wise not to lock your doors. Anyone can come in here."

"People will be in and out of the house all day today and it would be inconvenient to lock the doors and get up to unlock it every time someone rings the doorbell. This neighborhood is safe, and we've lived here for decades without a problem. In this neighborhood, we look out for each other." The driver had placed his load down in front of us and returned to the car while we discussed the merits of locked doors versus friendly neighbors. I pushed the bundle of stuff with my foot until I got to a point where I could drop my load in the living room.

"Lecia and Kade." Her mother came rushing to greet us with her arms outstretched. "Mi nieto." Papi came out behind her and stood over his wife, who had taken Miles out of Lecia's arms and was cradling him as they looked down at him.

"Nuestro primer nieto," *our first grandchild.* "Marisela, this is a great day for our family. Our daughter and her husband have come home with their first child. We must celebrate." Marisela gave Miles to Papi, and Papi sat down to look at him, though he hadn't opened his eyes yet.

"Watch his head Aridio," she warned as Miles' head snapped back, prompting him to yell in protest at the sudden movement. Lecia's sister came into the room and sat next to Papi.

"Let me hold him—my first sobrino." Papi passed Miles over to Marissa and she delivered kisses on his chubby cheeks. Soon afterwards, the room overflowed with relatives who had come to see Miles for the first time.

"Remember everyone, he's a newborn, so we'll need to let him get a little older and bigger before we start passing him around." Lecia took him from her sister and cradled him in her arms while nodding her head in agreement with Marissa that Miles would not be passed around the room, which was overflowing with twenty to thirty relatives.

"The food is ready, so why don't you all join me in the dining room to begin our feast to celebrate mi nieto's homecoming." She waved her hands and ushered everyone out of the room except for me, Lecia, and Aridio, who remained seated to rest his leg. He was still healing from the fall several months ago.

"Let me see the baby Lecia." Senora Lydia looked over at Miles, who was blinking and about to open his eyes.

"What a beautiful child. Marisela said you weren't going to pass him around, but I'm like an aunt to you and I've known your family since before you were born. Hand him to me." Lecia was about to respond to her but I intervened.

"Senora Lydia, if we let you sit with him, others will be offended, so it's best, at least for now, that we limit those holding him to immediate family." She pursed her lips as if she were sucking on that sour lemon.

"Of course, whatever you say Kaiden Moore. You're his father and I will respect your wishes."

"Yes, Lydia, Cade is Miles' father and his wishes should be respected. I also told you Lecia didn't think it was wise to pass him around just yet." Marisela had returned to the room and took a seat.

"I understand he's a newborn, but Lecia, you're aware I know how to take care of a baby, don't you? I'm not just anybody. I'm as much your aunt, at least in spirit, as your tia Maria is."

"The fact that he was born early is only one reason why you shouldn't hold him, Senora Lydia." Lecia snapped.

"Well, what's the other reason Lecia; please tell me." She leaned forward to listen to Lecia's explanation and I also leaned forward, as I was uncertain what she planned to say.

"It's possible Mario has evaded capture for so long because you're helping him. You're aware he planned my baby's kidnapping, aren't you? He stole my baby from me." She spoke through her teeth, seething with anger, and startled Miles awake as she rocked him.

"Waaah!" he cried out, and she looked at him, diverting her attention from Senora Lydia but not before she squinted and shot daggers at her. *It's on now.* I sat back to witness the showdown.

"Yes, Marco told me about the rumors going around about Mario, but it can't be true. I know my son and he would never do such an evil thing."

"So, you're not denying that you helped him escape? Maybe helping him to get back to the Dominican?"

"Lecia, you're a mother now and someday you'll understand that good mothers do anything to help their children."

"Good mothers don't help their children do things that are wrong. I understand that already Senora."

"Lydia, why do you think me and Aridio would lie about Mario? We also believe he was involved in the kidnapping," Marisela joined in.

"Marisela, I think you and Aridio are blinded by the wealth and power of the Moore family and Mario is their scapegoat. I appreciate the pain they must have felt when the baby was taken, but I know Mario, and you two know him also. It wasn't that long ago, Aridio, that you disliked Cade and didn't want Lecia to marry him. What's changed? You don't think that maybe Cade and his family are lying to get both of my sons out of the way? Maybe they resent Marco because he was her first love and hurting Mario hurts Marco?"

I couldn't contain myself any longer. This woman was out of her damn mind.

"Senora Lydia, with all due respect, I'm not jealous of Marco and I will never be jealous of any of your sons. Your ideas are absurd and at the very least kind of twisted. I don't hold you responsible for your son's behavior, but let me make it clear, he's responsible for my son's kidnapping and terrorizing my wife. He'll pay for his crimes as well as all of those involved in denying us justice by harboring a fugitive."

It took everything I had to not mention the video. I decided it was best to let her hold on to her delusions about her son and hope she'd get sloppy in her zeal for vindication and lead me straight to him.

She didn't say anything further, and I knew it was difficult for Aridio and Marisela to continue to act as if they were comfortable with continuing the relationship with Lydia Rodriguez. I had asked them and Lecia to play it cool and let me handle it.

"Lydia, you're right that I had reservations about Cade when I didn't know him, but that's in the past. Cade has proven me wrong, and he's Lecia's husband, a respected member of this family and the father of my grandson. I suggest you treat him with respect and we'll all agree to disagree," Papi piped in, trying to calm the situation.

Miles resumed crying, so I unzipped the baby bag and gave Lecia a blanket to drape over her shoulder so that she could nurse him under the cover. Her parents and Senora Lydia's mouths dropped open as she unbuttoned her shirt and placed Miles at her breast to quiet him.

"Lecia, don't you want to nurse him in the bedroom in private? Her mother leaned forward to block her father's view while he looked away. "Things are different with your generation, but you have many male relatives in the house and their wives may feel a little uncomfortable."

"Mami, it's perfectly natural to nurse a child, but I'll go to one of the bedrooms if you wish." She heard the pop as Miles released her nipple and resumed sleeping.

"He's asleep." She handed him to me to burp him while she buttoned her shirt. Miles was six weeks old and we had rehearsed the routine so many times in places that didn't have private stations for nursing babies that we were experts by now. Lively bachata music was playing now, and I began moving my head to the music while rubbing Miles' back.

"Give him to me, Lecia, while you and Cade go get something to eat. Your wishes will be respected, and I'll make sure of that. Don't worry," she looked at Senora Lydia and reached for the baby.

"That's a good idea and I'm hungry. We'll eat then, my dear wife, I challenge you to dance with me and show me what you got." I had taken lessons from Dana since Lecia loved the merengue and to dance to bachata music.

"I don't know if I feel like dancing right now." She looked over at Miles fast asleep in his grandmother's arms.

Marisela tried to reassure her. "He'll be fine Lecia, and he'll be with me until I return him to your arms. Go with Cade and enjoy yourself. I've prepared some of your favorite foods. See what we have, eat a little, then come back here if you wish. I'll be waiting for you here since the music is a little too loud for the baby's tender ears."

"You're right Mami, but you shouldn't have gone to so much trouble."

"Check his bag Marisela. I think I remembered to pack Miles' earphones." I extended my hand to Lecia to encourage her to join me.

"Come on, chicken. Afraid I'll embarrass you with my dancing skills?"

"I could show you a few dance moves in my sleep." She grabbed my hand and led me to the dining room, filled with chicken, fish, and beef dishes. We enjoyed eating off the same plate, and I challenged her to a dance again as she found it difficult to resist the hot rhythms of the bongos and guitar and the swaying of bodies to the bachata.

"I'll show you no mercy buddy." Lecia moved to the floor and began her classic moves of the merengue. She ran her hands through her hair, and it wasn't long before she was moving her hips from side to side in a lively and sensual dance. She opened her mouth in surprise that I was able to keep up with her, and I showed her some moves of my own. I took her into my arms and she began whispering in my ear.

"Those lessons have paid off. You're a really, good dancer Cade. I'm impressed."

"Thanks, and I hope we get lucky too." She leaned back and looked into my eyes.

"What are you talking about?"

"I hope Senora Lydia tries to contact Mario while we're here in North Carolina. Our security has tapped her phone and we should be able to trace the call if she tries to contact him."

"Cade, I don't want you to try to trap Mario. He's probably desperate and dangerous."

"He's no more desperate than I am to have him pay for his crime." We finished the dance and she grabbed my hand to head out the door while Papi was coming into the room with two guitars.

"Come on Cade, let's show these people how to make music." I grabbed one of the guitars and sat in the chair next to Papi. Other members of the family joined us in the circle with their instruments and began playing to the beat. I had played with Papi several times and knew some of his favorites. We played while others joined us singing. Marisela came in the room with Miles wearing earphones and sat next to Lecia, who was smiling as she held onto Miles' little fingers.

Lecia had gotten what she wanted and deserved. She had returned home with our son, who was safe and surrounded by the love of family.

CHAPTER SEVENTEEN

I woke up early and eased out of bed while Lecia turned over, still asleep. It had taken a lot of discussion to convince her to let Miles sleep in the bedroom next to us, and I didn't want anything to go wrong and derail my plans to have him sleep in his nursery when we returned to New York. I hadn't heard him stirring over the monitor, so I went next door to check on him after washing up. I grabbed my phone before tiptoeing out of the room, making sure not to wake Lecia since she was still tired from a night of partying with her family.

Right away, things felt off after I opened the door to his room. The red light on his baby monitor was off and, although sunlight shone into the room and brightened the space, the little bear nightlight had been unplugged. I could see portions of his rumpled blanket peeking above the side of his bassinette and my legs got weak. Lecia never wrapped him in a blanket at night, and the last I saw him, he was in his onesie sleeper.

My eyes widened, my heart was racing, and it was hard to catch my breath as I looked in the empty bassinette and he was gone! There was nothing in his bassinette except for his favorite bunny, covered with the blanket—no Lecia thought it was his favorite—sitting at the foot of the mattress.

Calm down. He's in the house somewhere. I'll start in the kitchen.

I stumbled out of the room on my way to the kitchen. Rationally, I knew he was nearby, but I was in five-alarm-fire mode until I got to the kitchen.

There was the smell of pancakes and the table had been set with a dome-covered warming plate in the center, but no one was there. I noticed the door to the deck and seating area off the kitchen was left ajar, and I was frantic as I raced to the door. Even though I was blinded by the bright sun, I could see Vincent cradling something in his arms. *Lord, let it be Miles in his arms.*

"Vincent, do you have Miles?" I was almost out of breath and needed to sit down, but I leaned against the door frame for support.

He turned around and had Miles in a sling resting against his chest.

"Yes, me and little buddy were just enjoying the morning sun. Everything ok bro? You look a little distressed."

"Good, good morning." I came forward and rubbed his head while he slept in the sling; I had to reassure myself through touch it was him and I could relax knowing he was alright.

"You should get one of these things Cade. I used it a lot when the twins were babies and they really come in handy. I got up early and made some pancakes. Let's go inside and get some; there's food on the table and in the warmer on the stove."

"I think I'll have some coffee first." I needed time to distance myself from my panicked feelings, still evident by my shaking hands as I tried to pour a cup of coffee. "Was Miles fussing and that's why you got him?" I went back to the table and took a seat while Vincent was already at the table bottle feeding Miles with one hand and eating his pancakes with the other.

"Oh, that's why you look a little spooked." He put his fork down on his plate. "I didn't think…I'm sorry. It hasn't been that long since you and Lecia had to live through a nightmare and I was only thinking about allowing the two of you to sleep in and for me to get in some time with my favorite nephew and godson. Dana and I have had our position lowered on the totem pole when it has come to spending time with him this weekend thanks to our parents and grandmother."

"Yes, and it seems at times like Lecia and I have had to make an appointment to be with our son between the time spent here and with her family."

"Miles was waking up when I went to get him, so I brought him in here to help me make the pancakes and, if you don't mind, I'll take him to Dana to change him and dress him. We'll probably leave later today, and she wanted some time with him before we left."

"I'm sure Lecia will appreciate the help, but I'd better tell her before she freaks out."

Lexie, Vincent and Dana's daughter, currently six years old, came running into the kitchen and shoved her recorder in her father's face. "Daddy, I need to show you something now. My music isn't working, and I won't be able to practice my ballet without my music."

"Lexie, we have plenty of time to fix your recorder or get you a new one. Your recital is a week from now and I need to take Miles to your mother, alright?"

"It's not alright Daddy. You always make me wait." She frowned and placed her hands across her chest in a huff.

"Lexie, enough. I'll be right back." He got up and left the room with Miles while I sighed, unsure how to pick up the pieces.

"Want some pancakes?" I pulled out a chair and motioned for her to sit beside me.

"I'm not hungry," she responded and placed her head on her folded hands resting on the table. She didn't resist me patting and kissing the back of her head.

"I would appreciate it if you would eat a little with me, so I won't have to eat alone."

"Alright, I'll do it for you." I got up and fixed us a plate. We had both had to deal with a little distress this morning and a few pancakes was sure to be a cure. I gave her a fork and we both dug in.

"Oh, these are good. Your dad makes the best pancakes."

"Yes, he does. He tells us all the time that he does it because he loves us but sometimes I don't think he has time for all of us, especially me." She poured the syrup on her pancakes and took a bite while swinging her feet in delight despite her frustration earlier. I took another bite and put my fork down before pulling my phone from my pocket.

"Does this look like a daddy who doesn't have time for his princess?" She grabbed my phone with her sticky fingers and scrolled through pages of pictures of her. "Your dad has always acted from the day you were born as if you were a precious jewel to him."

"Daddy likes babies," she shrugged and brushed off my comments.

"Well, with you little Lexie, it was different." She looked up at me this time, staring and intent on hearing my answer.

"You were his first little girl, his princess, and as long as you live you'll always be his first girl, and that's special."

"Thanks Uncle Cade," she got up and hugged me. "I guess I feel better." She went to the fridge and pulled out a small container of milk. "Want some?"

"No thanks." I turned and saw Lecia entering the room, still in her robe.

"Good morning," she greeted us and yawned while looking around the kitchen.

"Good morning Aunt Lecia," Lexie responded from the corner of the room where she was busy getting a plastic glass for her milk.

"Be careful princess. Need some help?"

"No Uncle Cade, I've got it."

"Where's Miles?" she asked as I got up and pulled out a chair for her.

"I was on my way to tell you he's with Vincent and Dana. They're taking care of him, so you could sleep in. Are you okay?"

"I'm fine. Why do you ask?"

"It didn't freak you out when you looked into his bassinette and didn't see him in there?"

She cocked her head to the side and gazed inward before responding.

"I guess not because I feel safe here and I know Miles is safe here."

"It's safe here Aunt Lecia," Lexie agreed as she walked slowly back to the table with her glass of milk. "I feel safe here, and it's fun coming to Grammie's house."

"Yes, it is my sweet Lexie." Lecia bent over her and gave her a kiss on top of her head.

"Want some pancakes babe?"

"No thank you. I think I'm going to go back to bed for a little bit. Miles and I are going to be at my parents' house for most of the day while you're at the studio downtown. I'll meet you there this evening after I get back from my doctor's appointment so that we can have our date night. Have a great day." She came over and planted a kiss on my lips before retreating to the bedroom.

"Alright princess, what can Daddy do for you? And thanks for your patience my precious girl." He came into the kitchen and went directly to the seat beside Lexie. She got up and crawled into his lap after finishing her pancakes and milk.

"You're welcome Daddy, but I can wait."

"I'm here for you princess. Let me look at your recorder." He grabbed it off the table and unjammed the play and pause buttons. The music started playing and they both broke out in bright smiles.

"There, problem solved princess."

"You're the best Daddy, and you make really good pancakes." She planted a kiss on his cheek.

"Thanks sweetheart. I'll do anything to keep you happy. So, you're not angry with me anymore?"

"No, I'm not, and I have to go practice. Bye Daddy and Uncle Cade." She kissed him again and climbed off his lap before skipping out of the room.

"You must have said something to her. Usually she pouts longer and is irritable Lexie before my sweet Lexie returns."

"I just showed her the hundreds of pictures of her you've sent me over the years—and it didn't hurt that the pancakes were really good."

"Really, I sent you hundreds of pictures?" I showed him the pictures as I scrolled through them.

"Hundreds, and that was the amount of pictures of just one of your four kids. I've had to store most of the pictures in the cloud to have some space on my phone." We shared a laugh.

"I guess I do go overboard when it comes to the kids, and I'm sure you'll be the same way with Miles. He's one lucky little boy and it amazes me that he can yell on key. I think he's got your musical talent."

"Lecia's dad is a musician too, and he probably has gotten it from both sides of the family."

"He's one lucky little boy to have you as a father."

"Thanks bro." My face felt flushed and my chest expanded with his words of encouragement. My father and my brother were great fathers and examples of what I expected of myself. "You're a great father, and that means a lot to me coming from you—a whole lot."

We looked at each other as we both realized there was no more we needed to say about the subject. After a moment of awkward silence, I cleared my throat before attempting small talk.

"It's good being home again with all of us under the same roof. Lecia has been more relaxed knowing that Miles is safe here among his extended family."

"I wasn't sure if I needed to share this with you Cade, because I didn't want to get your hopes up, but there are strong signals coming from the contractors in the Caribbean that a man fitting Mario's description has been spotted at

Mountain Estates in Haiti and Puerto Rico that are owned by the drug cartel.

"What's he doing there?" I rubbed the sides of my coffee cup.

"From what I have reviewed, it seems Mario is a former classmate of Jean Claude Malveaux, who was born in Haiti, but his family emigrated to Puerto Rico and then to North Carolina. Malveaux's family is old money—old drug money. They don't have the power they once had, but he's got enough influence with several government officials in the Caribbean to run an operation and provide security to his friends who are on the run. Mario has grown a beard and put on a few pounds, but we're certain the new guy is him. His affiliations with a cartel explain how he was able to get away, but we're going to get the bastard."

"Then what?" I looked at Vincent. I didn't have blood on my hands and I wasn't certain about him.

"As I said before, The Network has an interest in him and will deal with him as they choose." I ran my hands through my hair.

"I know I want him caught, and I need to face him before I decide what *I* want to do."

"Let's talk about this later. I don't need to have Dana hear me talking about the Network."

"Thanks for your help Vincent. I need to get dressed so I can get to the studio to lay down a few tracks."

"Sure, Cade. We can catch up with each other later today. You'd better go before the folks start complaining we're both working too hard and should spend more time with the family."

"You're right." I quickly pushed the chair away from the table. "See ya."

Act I. The Seed on FIre

I returned home from the studio and was spending some time in my mother's home office trying to finish the day's work after a long session of practicing with the band. I had spoken to Lecia by phone and she'd told me of her plans to go to bed early after spending a long day at her parents' home. As I entered the house, my phone buzzed, and I looked at the phone before accepting the call from my personal security chief.

"Good evening. I'm calling to give you an update on the Rodriguez family. Mrs. Rodriguez has not attempted to call her son since we started tracking her calls, nor has she received calls from anyone other than her usual contacts. She may be delusional about her son's innocence, but she's not dumb."

"Stay on it. My brother is working on the case with some of his friends in international intelligence and I'm hoping for a break in the case soon."

"Don't worry boss. I'll stay on it until we get the bastard."

"I know you will. Bye."

It was late, and I checked my messages; there was one from the hotel confirming our room reservation for tomorrow. I hoped Lecia's doctor's appointment would go well and I would get a green light for a night of love. I was craving her body, but first things first, I had an album to finish and I needed the nerve to tell her about the band's plans for a year of touring in the next six months. I blew out a breath and tried to focus on the task at hand as I took a seat at the desk.

Lecia had inspired me to write the lyrics to a song about superpowers after she informed me that I was her Superhombre, but I couldn't get past the mental block to compose the music to accompany the lyrics. I spoke the lyrics to the first verse out loud, hoping a tune would come to mind.

What is your Superpower?
Healing plants flourished
in a beautiful garden.
Each bearing gorgeous flowers.
Some delicate, some bold
Flowers whose beauty
Worth more than silver and gold.

Only the gardener knew the secrets
of these magical flowers.
He guarded and protected them,
for they conveyed Superpowers.

One hour later, there was still no music in my head, and the computer screen was blank except for the blinking cursor taunting me. I powered off the screen with a firm press of my index finger against the power button and grew more irritated as the message popped up, "Do you want to save this?"

"Hell no. There's nothing to save."

I got out of my chair and went to our bedroom to snuggle against Lecia's warm body.

CHAPTER EIGHTEEN

Sometimes working through a creative block with paper instead of on the computer was what I needed to finish a song, but nothing was working today. I thought I had cleared my head from thoughts about Mario, at least for the time being but my underlying anger was probably interfering with my creative process. I sat at my desk shaking my head locked in an internal battle that something, anything would come across my mind, but nothing filled the space in my brain.

I placed my head in my hands, knowing I was fighting it and that I had never won a battle when I fought the process instead of letting my creativity flow. Balling up the blank sheet of music before me, I threw it at the wall near the door.

"Whoa," Lecia sideswiped the wad of paper coming her way.

"Were you trying to strike me out?" She came into my office and gave me a kiss on the lips. I hugged her and inhaled her sweet scent.

"Is everything alright?" She stroked my hair while I kept my arms around her waist and leaned in.

"I need to ask you the same thing. How was your doctor's appointment?"

"It went well, and she cleared me for sex." I hugged her tighter and kissed her shirt, pressing my face against her abdomen.

"That's the best news I've had today." I loosened her from my embrace and she took a seat near me. "You're here early Lecia. Are you hungry and want to go to dinner sooner than we planned?"

"No, I'm fine. I thought I would catch a little of your practice session with the guys before we went to dinner. Where's everybody?"

"They're on a break, and the guys went out to dinner to get out of the studio. Things just weren't flowing today, and we all needed to get away."

"I see, so why are you struggling over the music? You still haven't been able to move past your mental block?"

"No I haven't." I looked up at her, observing her facial features a little closer.

"Did you change your hair?"

"It's curled a little tighter, but that's it?"

"Are you wearing different makeup?"

"Nope, very little makeup. Since I had Miles I don't use that much because I don't want it to get on him and irritate his skin."

"Oh, I see, but something's different." I got up, closed the door, and made sure it was locked before assisting her to her feet so that I could gaze a little closer at her.

"I think you haven't seen me look rested in a long time and maybe you're seeing me through clearer lens because you're also rested. It has been good being here."

"Yes, it has been." I placed my greedy tongue in her mouth and let all the tension flow out of my mind and into my dick. "You have such a calming effect on me Lecia." I pressed my erection against her groin.

"Not all of you is relaxed." I guided her hand to my crotch, excited to feel her touch.

"All of me doesn't need to be relaxed if I'm to succeed with the plans I have for you."

"Cade, the band will be back soon. Don't start something you can't finish." I planted kisses down the side of her neck and placed my head down into her cleavage. She had on a black A-line dress with an exposed zipper running down the back. I placed my hands behind her back and listened to the sound of the zipper as I slowly pulled it down to the small of her spine. Leaning over her, I planted kisses on one shoulder and then the other as I helped her out of her dress, leaving her clad in her black-laced bra, matching underwear, and thigh-high stockings along with her pumps. She extended her arm in search of the lamp on my desk.

"What are trying to do?" I wasn't sure what on my desk had her attention.

"I'm trying to turn off the lights babe." She turned her head and I grabbed her hand to stop her from reaching the lamp.

"Why do we need to turn off the lights? Seeing you like this is such a visual turn on, Lecia. I noticed you've been hiding your body lately from me, and that makes me feel bad. I don't understand—well, on some level I do, but it doesn't make me happy that you're depriving me of the visual pleasure only your body can give me."

"You think it's pleasurable having a little more weight around your middle? My body has changed after having the baby." I saw the sadness in her eyes.

"Yes, it's changed, but not for the worse Lecia. Looking at your body is something I look forward to every night, and more so after the baby. I love you so much and my love for you is blind to any blemishes you think you have. That's why I use the desires of my heart and my privilege to touch you and caress you as my true guide."

"I know you love me, and I also know you're sex starved Cade, but give me time to get used to my new body. You're not about to tell me you like me a little heavier, are you?" She looked away from me.

I went in a little closer, lifted her chin, and tucked a lock of her hair behind her ear.

"What I'll tell you is that I'll be there to support you in your journey. If you want to change your diet, I'll change my diet. I'll be your exercise buddy if you need one, and I'll watch Miles when you want time to yourself. Whatever you need, as long as you promise to stop hiding from me. I want to celebrate your body, not criticize it."

"I appreciate that, and I'm willing to do anything to make this a good night for you, but I'm not feeling as sexy as I used to feel."

I backed away from her and lifted my shirt over my head, exposing my pecks, then undid my pants and pulled them down before kicking off my shoes.

"Feeling any sexier now?" Her eyes dilated, and she licked her lips.

"I'm getting there." She sighed and cupped the back of her neck. "It's getting a little warm in here, or is it just me?"

"Maybe you should get out of those stocking and shoes. That might help." I rubbed my erection, causing my boxers to stretch out in front of me, and moved closer to her as she came out of her clothes.

"Did you say you were worried about this part of your body?" I leaned over and kissed her belly. "This part that nurtured and protected my son, the greatest gift you could have ever given me, while he grew inside you?" She nodded.

"It has a few stretch marks on it now." She lowered her head again and I lifted her chin and placed a kiss on her lips.

"Are you talking about the little enticing arrows leading down to my most favorite XX spot? The oasis of warm, moist pleasure? I'm getting more excited thinking about sinking myself into you right now." I placed her hand on my hard on.

"Your body has only become more beautiful to me." I undid her bra and threw it on the floor and took my time sucking each nipple, drawing out her nectar, which was milder and sweeter than the cold milk I drank from the fridge. "Now that's more satisfying than milk from my favorite cup. I squeezed her breast again and drew out more of the milky fluid.

"Are you getting your sexy back babe?" She pulled down her panties.

"Yes, I think that did it." Placing her arms around my neck, she drew me nearer and I pulled down my boxers before she wrapped her legs around my waist. I lifted her up and took her to the couch before laying her down and sinking myself deep inside her wet folds.

"Thank you, Cade, for loving me and refusing to see my flaws." She panted and gave in to my gentle thrusting inside her.

"You have no flaws I can see baby. Let's just feel the joy and give in to our pleasures. Am I making you feel good?"

"Yes baby. I love you so much and I lose myself in you." I placed her hand over my heart.

"Feel what you do to me babe." My heart was thumping, and I was starting to break out in sweat as I looked at her body moving beneath me.

"I feel your heart Cade." It skipped a beat as I plunged my tongue into her mouth and came up for breath to rest my ear at her lips while I kept thrusting inside her.

"I. Love. You, Cade." She knew those words drove me wild when we made love, and I wasn't sure if it was the huskiness in her voice and the angle of her body as she rotated her hips that drove me over the edge, but I began thrusting with a frenzied pace until we found our release.

She gulped in deep breaths as she tried to recover from her orgasm.

"That was so good Cade."

"Yes it was. You still got it girl," I panted in reply.

"You still got it." I rested my head on her shoulder. I was one happy man until a few minutes later when a knock on the door and the voice of my trumpet player interrupted my moment of bliss.

"Cade, we're back. Let's try to knock out that last number before we call it a night."

"Alright, I'll be right out." I called out and Lecia smiled at me.

"Time to get back to work Cade, but I think you've already scored a knockout."

I kissed her and got up off the couch to find my clothes.

"This shouldn't take too long, then we can get something to eat and pick back up where we left off."

"Take your time and I'll check on our reservation. The restaurant will probably be okay if we don't get there right on time." I nodded and pulled my pants over my hips, going commando.

"I'll be right back soon but before I leave, come and lock the door behind me until you get your clothes back on." I stayed outside the door until after I heard the click of the lock.

"Cade, do you think you're ready to finish this session or should we just try it again tomorrow?" Jared Jackson, my longtime friend and producer asked from the recording booth.

"No, I think I've got this. Let's start from the top and I think I'm going to improvise some portions of the track if that's alright with the band?" I looked around at the nods from my band, Fortune. "I don't think they'll have problems following me and we can see how this take works out."

I positioned the headset and raised my fingers in a silent count, *and a 1, 2, 3* and started playing my sax. I felt from the first note that I was in the zone and the band was playing well with me. There was a return to joy as I felt I was not only hearing the music but feeling it as well. The eyes of the other members of my quartet were transfixed on me as I was able to hit higher notes and held them longer than I had been able to in the session hours before.

My creative block had lifted, and I smiled knowing that the recording session was finally going well. Feeling grateful and delighted by the music we were creating, my feet were moving as I pointed first to Mike on keyboard, letting him display his talent in a solo portion, followed by Hasan Mehdi, who was a genius on multiple instruments. His improvised rendition of the piece on cello was stunning, and Rudolph Wolfman, "Wolf," could have brought any house down with his high-energy performance on drums. I closed out the set coming back in on the sax before we hit a crescendo of notes and ended the recording of the set.

"Damn, now that's what I'm talking about," Jared yelled out over the mic from the recording booth and the engineer gave us the thumbs up.

"Cade, I don't know what got into you, but I don't think we could improve upon that track. I'm going to listen to it again tonight before signing off on it, but I think you all can call it a wrap."

Lecia came into the room just as we were putting away our instruments.

"Hi guys. I was listening to that last take and it was fantastic. I will be surprised if it isn't another hit. Cade, you were wonderful." She leaned in and gave me a kiss.

"Hi Lecia, how long have you been here?" asked Mike, my friend since childhood and an original member of the group.

"About an hour. I was in the office with Cade waiting for you all to return from dinner. How have you been?"

"I've been great, and it's good to see you again. Wolf and I are having a party at his place with some of the guys who usually tour with us later tonight. Why don't you and Cade join us?"

"Mike, Lecia and I have a date night planned. We haven't gotten out much since she delivered Miles."

"I was just thinking it would be good to get back together with the gang. Some of the girls will be there and I'm sure they would love seeing you and Lecia again. I'll text you the address to Wolf's place here in Charlotte."

"I can't make any promises that we'll be there." I was looking forward to a night with Lecia.

"Cool." He gave Lecia a friendly hug and walked off to join the other members of the band who had packed up and were in the booth with Jared.

Lecia leaned over again and kept her voice low. "Cade, my dress is wrinkled, and I'm probably dressed too conservatively for a party."

"I brought a bag with a change of clothes for you." She raised an eyebrow. "Don't worry about it. Dana packed the bag with an outfit and accessories for you for an evening of partying. I thought we could do something together before we went to the hotel."

"You want to stay out all night?" She shook her head slightly and her mouth twisted in disapproval.

"My parents will be home and they were excited to spend the evening with Miles, so I thought we could at least play it by ear and see how the night goes since we won't have their help next week. Why don't you go change, while I finish things with the band before we go? Dana told me to tell you to wear your hair up since the outfit would look better with an updo."

"Well, since you went to the trouble of making a reservation for dinner and a party for two afterwards, I agree, we should just see how it goes. I'll be right back after I've changed."

"I'll be here waiting." I patted her on the behind. "Don't make me wait too long?" She looked over her shoulder and gave me a side-eyed glance and a sly smile. She was out of earshot when Mike spoke to me over the mic in the booth.

"There's a consensus among us that you got laid while we were gone and that's what opened up that creative vibe. It was clear something had changed."

Looking in the direction of the booth, I smiled and shot them the finger. "Do I detect some jealousy, Mike, that I have a fine wife?" I spoke into the mic.

"No disagreement there buddy. Your wife is fine." Mike smiled back at me and Jared turned the mic in his direction and began speaking.

"We just wanted to offer our thanks to her for saving us probably hours of time trying to get the perfect take. We're grateful that after she *allegedly* found a way to loosen up your tight ass, your creativity started flowing again."

"You know Lecia is my muse and that's all I'll admit to." She came back into the room with her hair twisted up into a ball and large hoop silver earrings glistening in her ears. Her tight-fitting black jeans and sequined silver and black top belied the fact she had given birth just six weeks ago. My gaze was broken by loud whistles coming over the speakers from all the members of the band and their applause. She bowed to her admirers and took her time walking to me in stiletto heels to give me a kiss.

"I must tell Dana thank you." I clicked off the mic on the headset around my neck, placed it on the mic stand so I wouldn't be overheard, and whispered into her ear.

"Are you still worried you haven't gotten your sexy back? How you look in that outfit and all the evidence from my earlier observations of your luscious body point to the contrary and should reassure you." I kissed her ear and portions of her neck.

"Thank you, sweetheart. You guys are great for raising a girl's confidence." She clicked the mic back on and spoke to the guys in the booth.

"We'll try to make it to the party tonight, ok?" They smiled back at her.

"Great, we need to get going and hope to see you there." Wolf waved goodbye.

"Lecia, we'd better get going too so we won't be late for our reservation at the restaurant." I grabbed my saxophone case and took her hand to walk to the limo waiting outside for us.

CHAPTER NINETEEN

"I'm glad you chose that restaurant. Is it new?"

"Yes, Vincent and Dana recommended it because it reminded them of one of their favorite restaurants in Harlem." I placed my drink in the cup holder in front of us in the limo, as we rode through the streets of downtown Charlotte.

"The food was a mix of nouveau Southern recipes lightened up for those of us who are calorie conscious." She patted her stomach and smiled. "Oh, I'm so full."

"And great dishes for some of us more concerned about the taste of our food than the calories. My dish tasted like it came out of my mother and grandmother's kitchens, and you know they are both good cooks," I added as she sat in my embrace while we rode to the party. She laughed and touched my shoulder.

"You know what? Now that you mention the restaurant in Harlem, I remember why our server seemed so familiar to me. She reminded me of your friend Flo at the restaurant in New York. She served us on our first date—if you want to call it our first date."

"And now here we are. Married with a son and out on a date to commemorate your return to the life of a sexually active women. Speaking of our son, should you have had even that small glass of wine since you're breastfeeding Miles?" Despite my attempts to tread with caution, she leaned forward and pulled out of my embrace.

"Are you insinuating I would do anything to hurt my child?"

"No, I'm not worried about you hurting Miles. I'm just asking because I don't know about these things. Did your doctor mention anything about alcohol?" I squirmed in my seat under her angry gaze.

"You shouldn't worry about my ability to care for my son, and of course, I discussed this with my doctor, even though as a pediatric nurse practitioner, you'll recall, I know about these things, so let me share it with you." We both took a breath and I extended my hand to take her back into my embrace.

"School me babe, I need to know." She came back into my arms without resisting my attempts to keep us physically close. I patted her head and kissed the side of her face.

"You're his father and I should appreciate your concerns. I'm sorry if I got a little offended about it, but I've been getting unsolicited advice about caring for Miles from my mother, your grandmother, and your mother. I'm sorry I projected my frustration onto you, but to answer your question, infrequent consumption of small amounts of alcohol is permissible if I'm careful. I knew I might have four ounces of wine, and to prepare for tonight, I pumped and stored enough milk for him. I won't have to nurse him from my breast for the next twenty-four hours and my body should have cleared all the alcohol in the next two to three hours, so yes, Miles is safe."

"Thank you for explaining it to me. I'm a musician, you'll recall, and not a medical professional." She laughed and relaxed as we continued our way.

"I'm having a good time Cade, and I'd like to thank you for all you've done to make this night special."

"Your pleasure is my pleasure, but I looked for the black negligee I love so much on you for tonight and I couldn't find it."

"I didn't pack it because I didn't think I could fit into it."

"You can wear it. I don't think you're seeing how breastfeeding and taking care of the baby is allowing you to return to your pre-pregnancy weight. You're beautiful to me Lecia, pregnant, post-pregnancy, and pregnant again. You'll always be beautiful to me."

"Wait a minute stud. I just gave birth to a baby and I'm not thinking about having another one any time soon."

"We didn't think we'd get pregnant on our honeymoon and we did."

"Touché." She grabbed her forehead. "And we've done it again without a condom."

"I placed my swimmers on noninvasive mode and they knew not to pierce any eggs."

"Stop playing Cade. This is serious."

"Stop stressing Lecia. We got caught up in the moment, but I have condoms and I promise it won't happen again until you're back on the pill."

"You aren't worried we could be having another baby?" She looked up at me.

"Being Miles' father has been one of the best things that has ever happened to me. You weren't worried about it the first time we got pregnant, and I'm not worried about it this time. We love each other, and we can get through anything together."

"You're right. We were born for each other. You and Miles are my blessings and I'm so grateful for the two of you. I'm not worried and I plan to have some fun. Are we almost there?"

"We're just moments away from Wolf's house." I wasn't convinced partying with the band tonight instead of enjoying each other's company was a good idea.

Wolf answered our knock and greeted us with wide eyes and his mouth opened in surprise.

"What? The ghost has graced us with his presence? It must have been Lecia who convinced you to come since you haven't partied with us, Cade, since you got married. Come on in."

"Whoa!" A mini-roar came from the crowd of partygoers as we entered the room. Mike and Pete Willingham came to greet us.

"Lecia, you know Mike, and this is Pete. We call him 'Pablo' Willingham. He accompanies us on tours to play the guitar while Medhi is on the cello. Medhi is our wonderkid and can play multiple instruments, but when we're touring he likes to stay on the cello." He extended his hand to Lecia.

"Pleased to meet you Lecia. I'm glad you came out to have some fun with us tonight and brought this guy along with you."

"I'm pleased to finally meet you. I understand you, Wolf, Mike, and Cade have known each other for years, but you've been involved in other projects over the last year?"

"Yeah, I made a mistake signing with another group, so I'm the unofficial fifth member of Cade's group Fortune."

"Hey Mike. Hey Wolf. Where's Gina and the girls?" Lecia spoke and waved at them.

"Hey Lecia. Glad you're both here and she'll be happy to see you. I think she's in the kitchen," Wolf answered and came forward to join us in the small circle near the door.

"Cade let's get you two something to drink." Mike placed his hand on my back and attempted to lead me to the bar.

"Nothing for me Mike, but I'd like to go and say hello to Gina." Lecia responded and looked around the room.

"The kitchen's over there, but first let me take your coats." Wolf pointed to the kitchen before extending his hand to take our coats.

"Cade, I'll be right back." I looked as she disappeared behind hinged kitchen doors swinging constantly with people moving in and out with food and drinks. I turned and followed Mike as we passed some folks I knew and others who were unfamiliar to me. I waved at everyone. I hadn't been aware of furtive gazes from other women since I met Lecia, but for some reason, these women caught my attention. *I need to loosen up, and a drink should help.*

"You want the usual?" Mike asked.

"Yeah, sounds good." My first gulp was a big one, but afterwards, I took my time swallowing the smooth liquor.

"This is some good scotch. Is this imported?"

"No, it's a Kentucky single malt Wolf and I have been crushing on. Glad you like it."

"Yeah, I think I'll need to get some for my bar." I wetted my lips and turned my head in the direction of a tap on my shoulder.

"Let's dance." Lecia had returned and was pulling me on the floor.

"Do you mind if we have a seat on the couch over there while I finish my drink before we start dancing?"

"Sure. That's what we did when I came to my first band party with you two years ago. I felt shy and out of place, but you were so patient and kind with me."

"I'm glad you saw it as me being kind and patient. I thought it was a great opportunity to cuddle with you on a couch together. You were so busy shying away from the crowd, you didn't notice how many kisses I stole from you."

"And maybe I did notice but didn't care that the most handsome and talented man in the room was kissing me." I placed my arm around her shoulder and walked with her to the couch. The music was good, and everyone seemed to be having a good time, but my mind was focused on her naked body moving to the music we would be creating later tonight. We sat cuddled in each other's arms through several songs, just watching couples dancing on the floor and having fun. Lecia reached over and whispered in my ear.

"I love you so much Cade, and my soul hasn't felt this uplifted and carefree in weeks. Our baby is safe and I'm here having fun with you. Our love has been a blessing to me, and I wish all women could be as happy as I am tonight." My chest expanded to accommodate my heart, swollen with love for my wife, because it wasn't just the soft whispers from her lips to my hearing that touched me, but it was the connection we were strengthening—one heart to the other. She kissed my lips again, and the unexpected hard thump in my chest and the warmth spreading throughout my body showed me she had the capacity to reach into me and touch my soul.

"You're my soulmate and the only one there will ever be for me. My happiness gets magnified every time I see you happy, and I'm one happy man with you in my arms right now." Wrapped up in each other's arms in our own little cocoon of love, I was comfortable nursing my drink and sitting on the couch with Lecia all night. My phone rang, and Vincent's number popped up on the screen.

"Hello Vincent. What's up?"

"Hello Cade, where are you? I hear a lot of music and voices in the background."

"Lecia and I are at a party." Lecia told me to say hello to him. "Lecia said hi."

"Tell her hi. I just needed to let you know I'm heading to the Caribbean on a job. Dana wants to bring the kids after I'm finished, and I wondered if you and Lecia wanted to come and bring Miles."

"I'll ask her and get back to you. Be safe bro'."

"We're going to do this. I'll call you soon, bye."

"Bye Vincent." I hung up the phone and reflected on what was about to happen—the sooner the better. I took a swallow of my drink as I got lost in my thoughts.

"Everything's alright Cade, with Vincent and his family?" Lecia rubbed my chest, bringing my awareness back to the action in the room.

"Yeah, yeah. Everything's fine. Vincent has an assignment in the Caribbean, and Dana wants to go down there after he finishes the job. He wondered if we could join them?"

"Dana told me about their plans, but I don't want to take Miles down there until he's older. You understand, don't you?"

"Sure baby. We can go later and maybe take your parents and Marissa with us."

"Really Cade?" She smiled and bounced in her seat, then turned my head and gave me a deep and longing kiss. I loved being Lecia's Superhombre. We broke our kiss and turned to look at the dancers enjoying themselves on the dance floor.

I took in a cleansing breath, as if a cloud had lifted from around me thanks to Vincent, and despite my desires to remain an observer of the action going on around us, Gina came across the room, an unwelcomed intruder, ending my personal party.

"Come on Lecia. It's time for the girls' dance." Gina got the attention of the DJ and pulled Lecia to the floor. The music changed to a more upbeat number, and as if he were about to play the siren song, the DJ called the women to the floor over the mic to start the dance for women only. The floor filled with women, some doing choreographed moves and others freestyling to their own beat.

"Hi Cade, let me steal this beautiful woman from you for a little bit." Lecia got up and left me exposed with an erection fully formed. She didn't notice it, but I looked up and a women I didn't know in a short black body dress was looking my way again, but she quickly looked away before our eyes locked on each other. I moved a pillow onto my lap until the bulge in my pants subsided while Lecia was on the floor revving up and bird calling with the other women.

"Ca-caw!" she threw her head back and smiled as she swayed her hips in a salsa.

Lecia with an alcohol-infused buzz was always uninhibited, and I didn't plan to share her visual delights with another man. My girl can do many things but handling her liquor after a long drought without it, wasn't one of them.

I was growing irritated as she garnered the attention of every man in the room, watching her move her chest and hips, exuding the heat of sensuality she kept hidden from others except me.

Act I. The Seed on FIre

Time to put an end to this. I placed my glass on the table next to the couch and walked to the floor after the second girls' only dance ended.

"DJ, can we slow this party down? I need to hold my girl right now." He faded out the song and replaced it with a slower number to the moans of some of the women and men.

What the hell? I'm using my bandleader privilege, and besides it's almost time for us to go.

"You do know you had the attention of almost every man in the room?" I moved her to the center of the room and swayed with her in my arms to the music.

"Does it matter if I only wanted the attention of the most handsome man in the room?"

"And who would that be?" I leaned back to look at her soulful brown eyes.

"What man stopped the music and is holding me right now?" I smiled and leaned back into her so that her head rested easily on my chest.

"I guess that would be me. You know I don't like sharing your attention with anyone over the age of one year old." We both laughed. "Lecia, this night is about us. Let's get out of here and spend the rest of the night together, just the two of us."

"You're not having fun?" She placed one hand on the side of my face.

"I'm just ready to go." My thoughts for a second went to the woman, who was again watching me in an unguarded moment and invading my privacy. The song ended, and I hoped Lecia would agree to get out of here.

"Let me check on Miles first and then we can begin saying goodbye to our hosts and the other guests."

"Miles is fine Lecia. Let's just grab our coats and say a quick goodbye." I didn't realize we were still in the middle of the floor plotting our escape until Gina came back to speak to us.

"Everything okay?" Gina placed her hand on Lecia's shoulder.

"We're going to need to leave to get back to the baby."

"Lecia, you can't possibly leave without showing us pictures of Miles."

"I have pictures in my purse, but I think Cade has a few in his wallet." I was grateful to place my hand in my pocket and gave Lecia my wallet while I quickly slipped both hands in my pockets to hide my growing erection.

"You can show Gina the pictures. There should be some in the corner pocket."

"Alright," she shrugged her shoulders and found the pictures and gave them to Gina while we moved away from the center of the dance floor.

"He's beautiful Lecia. When can we meet him? We were trying to give you all space, but we would love to drop by the apartment when we get back to New York."

"Sounds like a date, but I need a quiet space where I can make a call to check on him." Gina pointed in the direction of a room to the rear of the house and I tried not to roll my eyes.

"This shouldn't take long," she assured me, and with that, she and Gina left me, and I moved to the corner of the room to reposition myself. I looked up and again, there she was staring at me and making a move in my direction.

"Do you want to dance?" she asked and placed a hand on my forearm.

"No thank you." I moved to the side to add a little more space between us. I didn't know this woman and I had no intention of dancing with her.

"Oh, come on, don't be a downer." She pulled at my arm and I jerked away.

"What the hell is wrong with you? I said no!" I frowned and audibly blew out air while my chest heaved. Pablo came in between us and faced her.

"Didn't you hear the man? He said no."

She cocked her head to the side and blinked as if she still didn't get it. "He's been stalked before and he doesn't like women coming on to him. He's not one of us."

"Why didn't he say so?" and she walked away while Pablo turned to face me.

"Sorry about that Cade, but she didn't know you and Lecia aren't swingers. Wolf and Mike don't swing either, but they know some of us are and that we'll be getting together elsewhere after the party."

"What about Medhi?"

"You know straight as an arrow Hasan Medhi doesn't swing."

"You're right, Lecia and I don't do that, and I'm not judging you Pablo, but don't ever invite us to one of those get-togethers."

"We all understand that Cade. No one is interested in watching you fight every man in the room, so we get it that we'd better not invite you and Lecia. I've known you for years and man, you've been wound up tight as a cobra ready to strike since your baby was born. We all see it and I don't know what all went down, but I understand you and Lecia have gone through some things." The scowl faded from my face as Pablo shared his observations.

"We've been through a lot." I rubbed my head and noticed the hair on my arm standing up after Lecia unexpectantly came up behind me with our jackets and touched me.

"Gina said she thought something happened that upset you and caused you to raise your voice. Is everything alright?" She handed my jacket to me.

"I'm tired and I think we should go. I was just telling Pablo to give our regards to Wolf and Mike." I placed my hand at the small of her back, barely giving her a chance to put on her jacket and nudged her to the door with Pablo walking behind us.

"I'll let the rest of them know you had to leave, but I just need to know we're still cool."

"Yeah, we're cool, and I will call you later, perhaps tomorrow to set up a schedule for studio work in New York next week."

"Good, and I'll be waiting for your call."

"It was good to finally meet you Pablo, good night."

"Same here Lecia, and maybe I'll get to see that baby boy of yours. Goodnight." I rushed Lecia out to the hallway and pushed for the elevator.

"Look at me Cade. I know you and something is bothering you. What is it? Talk to me, please." I looked up at the numbers and noticed the elevator had stopped on a lower floor and was slowly making its way up to us.

"It was just too much, too soon I guess, and I hated seeing the men in there, salivating over you." I pressed the button again repeatedly and Lecia turned me around and came into my arms.

"You're not normally in barfight mode when it comes to other men looking at me, and I know for a fact you like when other men look at me as long as they don't touch me or disrespect me or you, so what else was it?" I tried to look away, but she turned my head to face her.

"This woman came over and kept on bugging me to dance with her, and I guess it sent me back into that headspace of wondering if I had my ego in check, I wouldn't have let things get out of control with Darlene and I would have seen the signs that Marco and his evil brother Mario thought they could take what was mine." She began kissing me just before the elevator finally came to our floor. Grateful it was empty, I loosened her embrace but kept a hold of her hand while I led her inside and pressed the button for the first floor.

"We've been through a lot Cade, and it's going to take time for us to heal." The door closed, and the car descended without stopping until we reached the first floor. We stepped out to the lobby, nicely appointed with contemporary furniture and designer light fixtures. The doorman stood outside ready to open the door, but I stopped just before we reached him.

"We'll need to give the driver a few minutes to get here since I didn't call him before we left the party. Sorry, I just needed to get out of there." I took the phone out of my pocket.

"Wait Cade, let's take a seat before you call him. There's nobody down here and we need to talk. There's a couch in the corner and can we sit for a few minutes if you don't mind?"

"Lecia, I just want to get out of here."

"Please Cade, just for a few minutes. We've been trying to run from our feelings for the last six weeks, and maybe it's time we turned and faced them." She left me standing in the middle of the lobby and went to the couch, motioning for me to join her. She wasn't going to be deterred from talking to me, so I went to her and took a seat.

"I don't know what you want me to say, but I'm willing to listen." I turned to give her my attention and shifted my position as I grew uncomfortable thinking about what she was going to say to me. I took some solace in the hope that since we were in a public place, the conversation wouldn't get too deep. I had been running from memories of watching her fade away from me as she escaped into a deep sleep in her hospital bed six weeks ago out of fear our son may not have been alive. I didn't want to go there. *I couldn't go there.*

I looked her in the eyes and a thick shroud of sadness descended upon me, threatening to engulf me and imprison me in my own personal hell. *Damn, she's going there and taking me with her.*

"I'll start then. Cade, I have times when I get so angry I think I'm going to lose it too. My heart starts racing and I feel so hot, I think I'm going to pass out, but I take deep breaths to steady myself. I have to face the fact that it wasn't that long ago I wanted to die."

"Lecia, I'm not sure I can handle this right here and now. It still hurts to think you stopped believing in me and you gave up on us—well really on me. You stopped believing I would do anything to bring our son home and that I would never stop until I found him. I know it was mostly the drugs that kept you out of it, but I felt you were slipping away from me emotionally." She placed her hand on my leg and sat up on the edge of the couch.

"Cade?" She let out a deep breath and continued speaking. "How could you think I gave up on you? I wanted to die because I didn't have the most precious gift that you've ever given to me—our son—and I thought at the time, the hole it created in my heart was too big to mend. I knew you wouldn't give up looking for him, but forgive me, I doubted that I could handle it if he wasn't still… I was also so eaten up with guilt, it was killing me."

"Lecia, I was hurting too, but I never doubted we would find him alive. I've never blamed you for his kidnapping, and I sure don't want to live without you."

"I know that, but I blamed myself and, on some level, I guess I still blame myself for missing the signs with Darlene and maybe for letting my ego celebrate that you wanted me and not her."

I took her into my arms and wiped away the single tear falling down her cheek.

"That's weird because I've been feeling for the last several weeks that you and Miles have paid for my sins of pride and vanity. I knew it wasn't normal or healthy how much attention Darlene was paying to me, and I didn't do anything about it."

"No Cade, it wasn't just you. I also knew Darlene was becoming obsessed with you, and I didn't say anything either." I hugged her tighter as an icy sensation coursing through my marrow made me shiver.

"Don't you realize my heart drew me to you and for me, it was you or no one? We were created for each other, and after you came into my life, I couldn't imagine living without you. Lecia, you're my inspiration and the cement that has held my life together. Before you, I was happy being a one-dimensional man, a musician. But because of your love, I've become a strong and fulfilled man and I couldn't risk trying to hold it down without you. We can't allow ourselves to even consider any reason to not be there for each other until our natural deaths—not even if we're suffering through one of life's shitstorms." We held on to each other and Lecia was the first to break the silence.

"Even if I had died, I could never completely leave you Cade. You have my heart forever and I freely leave it to you, even in death as my last testament. I never doubted that if I didn't make it because of my grief, my heart would still belong to you."

"Babe, I prefer having your heart beating and loving me in your sweet body." I smiled and tried to lighten it up between us. "We have to be patient with ourselves instead of blaming ourselves. We both have triggers we're now aware of, and we can't ever let our fears, other people, or circumstances drive us apart. We're two bodies but we share one heart." I took her onto my lap and rocked her.

"Pablo said he and the band members have noticed I've been wound tight, and I have to admit I've been barking at them more than I ever have. I think I'll take my time in the studio even if it takes a year to finish the album before I consider touring."

"Miles will be older then, Cade, and we can talk later about me and the baby joining you on the tour. Time will go by fast and the baby will keep me busy while we're on the road." I gave her the biggest hug, not realizing my own strength.

"Really Lecia. You're serious? You'll come on tour with me?" She grimaced as I held her and nodded.

"Too strong babe. You're coming on too strong." She tried wiggling out of my embrace.

"Sorry babe, I didn't mean to grab you so tight, but you've made me so happy. Let me call our driver, and I think we need to leave before people from the party come down and see us here. I'm not up for more questions at this time."

"I agree." Lecia smiled and I took my arms from around her to make the call.

"We can talk more at the hotel if you'd like." She lowered her eyes and, with her lips turned downward, she appeared to be gathering her thoughts before she spoke.

"I just want to go home and place my eyes on Miles. I know he's probably fine, but I want to be under the same roof with him." She looked at her fingers instead of up at me.

"Instead of in some hotel room with me?" I frowned.

"Yes, and in a familiar bed making new memories with you but…" she leaned in and whispered in my ear, "this time using a condom."

"I can do that." My frown lessened. "We'd better get up and go out front. I'm sure the driver is here by now." We stood up and I stopped her from walking forward.

"I need to leave a message for Pablo, telling him he can use the room if he wants to. If I offer it to him, he'll understand that I'm not judging him and we're okay. He's a great guitar player and I don't want the misunderstanding tonight to come between us or risk losing him before we go on tour next year." I finished the message and looked at her, so grateful for her love and support.

"Lecia, tell me you'll always love me, and you'll never give up on us. I certainly never will."

"I love you and when we get home, I plan to show you how much I love you. I promise, I'll never give up on us. We're strong together, and with love and patience, we'll get through this."

I took her by the hand and we walked to the car with a new resolve that the crimes against us wouldn't break us and, if anything, our adversity had made us stronger as two people committed to each other.

Michele Sims

CHAPTER TWENTY

Resting in bed two nights after our marathon night of sex, ending my sex drought, I listened to the steady drops of water from the shower accompanying Lecia's sweet melody as she sang in the bathroom. She hadn't done that since Miles was kidnapped, and it was good to hear her angelic voice. My phone on the desk rang and I picked it up.

"Hey Vincent."

"Hey Cade. I wish I had better news, but you needed to know this as soon as possible."

"Tell me. I'm by myself and Lecia is in the shower. She can't hear us."

"Cade, Mario evaded capture. We had him, and it was as if he was tipped off. I'm sorry that I couldn't personally bring him to justice, but this case has the highest level of attention at the Network now because one of our contractors was killed by Malveaux's people, and the Network always responds to the death of one of their own. The significance of this case has been elevated."

"I'm sorry to hear about the loss, but are you alright?"

"I'm fine and I'll be coming home soon. Dana and the kids are disappointed that they won't be coming to the islands, and I owe them a vacation. I'm sorry it didn't turn out differently, but I won't give up. I'll keep in contact. Talk to you soon."

"Bye Vincent." I kept my tone even, trying to hide my disappointment.

"Bye Cade."

I didn't notice Lecia had come into the room until she was hovering over me.

"I said give me my morning kiss Cade." I leaned in and planted a kiss on her lips and grabbed her shoulders, her skin still dewy fresh from her shower.

What could have gone wrong? A chill in the room caused goosebumps to rise on my chest, but as I looked into Lecia's brown eyes, I was warmed by their twinkle and by the glow of her smile.

"I love your smile babe." I took her into my arms and stroked her hair.

"Hmm, I like being in my man's arms. Let me warm you up." She snuggled into my chest, kissed me on my breastbone, and placed a hand above my heart.

"Lecia, did you talk to your mother about us possibly taking a trip to the Caribbean?"

"Yes, I did, and you should have seen how happy she and Papi were to think that someday soon they would return to the Dominican with their first grandchild. Cade, as far as my family is concerned, your shit doesn't stink."

My laugh was hearty, and I was grateful for Papi's approval.

"Cade, you have a growing fan base in the DR and they were bursting with pride to be related to a celebrity. Senora Rodriguez was there when I told them, and it looked as if she was sucking on that lemon again by the sour look on her face."

Lecia laughed and I tried to join her. *There it is. Mario was tipped off most likely by his mother.* Maybe not, but I didn't doubt it. Lecia stroked my chest while she spoke again.

"Do you know how much I love you? Every day, I'm blessed to love you and Miles just a little more. Some days I feel so happy, I think my heart is going to burst from joy."

"I love you more than life itself Lecia. You and Miles are my heart and I'll never stop loving this life I've been blessed to share with you."

No, I hadn't scored a victory knowing that Mario was on his way to face me and pay for his actions. But, that's today and there was always tomorrow. I knew someday I would have justice. I turned my full attention to Lecia and looked at her as I peeled her out of the towel to shower her with kisses and my love.

Michele Sims

ABOUT THE AUTHOR

Michele Sims is the "author-ego" of Deanna McNeil, MD and creator of the Moore Family Saga and the Fire God Series.

She loves writing hot love stories and women's fiction with multidimensional characters in multigenerational families. She is the recipient of the 2018 RSJ Aspiring Author Award and first runner up in the Introvert Press Poetry Contest for February 2018. She is a member of the LRWA, in Charleston, SC and the From The Heart Romance Writers' online group.

She lives in South Carolina with her husband who has been her soulmate and greatest cheerleader. She is the proud mother of two adult sons and the auntie to many loved ones. When she's not writing, she's trying to remember the importance of exercise, travelling, listening to different genres of music, and observing the wonders of life on this marvelous planet.

Thank you for reading my book, The Seed on Fire. If you enjoyed reading The Seed on Fire, please do me a favor and leave an honest review where you purchased it.

This book is Act I. of the prequels to The Fire God Tour and Act II. Playing with Fire is in the final phases of production. The Fire God Tour is the third book of the Fire God series but it also can be read as a standalone novel. The follow up novel to The Fire God Tour, Feeling the Heat will be available later in 2019.

Sign up at michelesims22.com with your email address for updates and giveaways.

Your support is appreciated.

Made in the USA
Columbia, SC
10 May 2019